THE HARDER THE FALL

Don't miss these other great books
by Lauren Barnholdt:

GIRL MEETS GHOST

THE HARDER THE FALL

LAUREN BARNHOLDT

Aladdin

NEW YORK LONDON TORONTO SYDNEY NEW DELHI

ALADDIN

An imprint of Simon & Schuster Children's Publishing Division
1230 Avenue of the Americas, New York, NY 10020
First Aladdin paperback edition March 2014
Text copyright © 2013 by Lauren Barnholdt
Cover illustration copyright © 2013 by Mary Lynn Blasutta
Series design by Lisa Vega
Cover design by Jeanine Henderson
All rights reserved, including the right of reproduction in whole or in part in any form.
ALADDIN is a trademark of Simon & Schuster, Inc., and related logo is a registered trademark of Simon & Schuster, Inc.
Also available in an Aladdin hardcover edition.
For information about special discounts for bulk purchases, please contact Simon & Schuster Special Sales at 1-866-506-1949 or business@simonandschuster.com.
The Simon & Schuster Speakers Bureau can bring authors to your live event. For more information or to book an event contact the Simon & Schuster Speakers Bureau at 1-866-248-3049 or visit our website at www.simonspeakers.com.
The text of this book was set in Minion.
Manufactured in the United States of America 0214 OFF
10 9 8 7 6 5 4 3 2 1
The Library of Congress has cataloged the hardcover edition as follows:
Barnholdt, Lauren.
The harder the fall / by Lauren Barnholdt. — First Aladdin hardcover edition.
p. cm. — (Girl meets ghost ; #2)
Summary: Kendall Williams talks to ghosts. This time it's Lyra who can't move on. Kendall's efforts to help her jeopardize her own relationships with her best friend and her boyfriend. And when Kendall finally reveals her secret ability, the results are devastating.
[1. Dead—Fiction. 2. Ghosts—Fiction. 3. Psychic ability—Fiction. 4. Middle schools—Fiction. 5. Schools—Fiction. 6. Mystery and detective stories.] I. Title.
PZ7.B2667Har 2013
[Fic]—dc23
2013000559
ISBN 978-1-4424-4247-4 (hc)
ISBN 978-1-4424-2147-9 (pbk)
ISBN 978-1-4424-2150-9 (eBook)

For Fiona Simpson,
who made working on this series the most fun ever

Acknowledgments

Thank you, thank you, thank you to:

Alyssa Eisner Henkin, for being the best agent I could imagine.

My mom and my sisters, for everything.

Kevin Cregg, for always being there.

And Aaron, my husband, for everything he is—I love you.

THE HARDER THE FALL

Chapter

1

Okay. Everything is going to be fine. I just need to stop obsessing over all the crazy things that are happening to me, and just relax. Of course, this is easier said than done.

I mean, let's look at a quick recap of my life, shall we?

1. I can see ghosts. That, in and of itself, is completely scandalous. I'm only twelve! How am I supposed to be expected to deal with the pressures of helping ghosts move on to the other side? It would be a lot of work for a grown-up, even. I have my hands full just trying to get through seventh grade.

2. I have my first maybe-almost boyfriend, Brandon Dunham. Brandon is sweet and smart and very cute, and he helps me with my math whenever I need it. He even gave me my very first kiss ever. He is pretty much the exact kind of person you would want to be your first crush. But still. Having a maybe-almost boyfriend can be stressful.

3. Brandon Dunham's mom died when he was younger, and now she is one of the ghosts I can see. (See number one, above.) When she first appeared a couple of weeks ago, she kept going on and on about how I should add myself to the green paper. I had no idea what that meant until a few days ago, when I was at Brandon's house studying with him and I looked at the green paper he's always carrying around in his backpack. And it turns out that the green paper is a list of things his mother wrote to him before she died—a list of things she thinks he should stay away from.

I quickly figured out that the fact that Mrs. Dunham wants me to put myself on the green paper means that she doesn't want me dating Brandon. But why? And how am

I going to help Mrs. Dunham move on if her unfinished business involves me staying away from her son?

Not that I think Brandon and I are, like, destined to be together or anything. I mean, we're only twelve. But still. You can see why I might be just a tad bit distracted, even though it's Sunday afternoon and I'm supposed to be relaxing and having a fun time, enjoying what's left of my weekend.

"What's going on?" my best friend Ellie asks me as we walk down Main Street. When the weather's nice, Ellie and I sometimes spend our Sundays down on Main Street. We buy fresh fruit salads and hot chocolates from Donelan's Market, look at all the different stationery at Poppy's Papeterie, and browse for cute hair accessories at Jasmine's Boutique.

(I'm a huge fan of hair accessories. I like to try to make sure my hairstyle matches my mood. Like today, for example. My hair is in lots of beachy waves around my shoulders, because I'm kind of feeling loose and up in the air.)

"Nothing's going on," I tell Ellie. Which is a lie. But I can't really tell her the truth. In fact, I can't tell anyone the truth. No one knows I can see ghosts. I wish I could tell Ellie, I really do. But I can't risk the fact that she might not believe me, or she might think that I'm crazy. I don't know what I would do if I ever lost her friendship.

"Are you sure?" Ellie asks. "Because you've been really—"

"Oh, look!" I exclaim, pointing to a storefront on the corner. "There's a new salon opening up." They have a huge sign in the window that says ALL NAIL POLISH 50% OFF.

"Don't change the subject," Ellie says as I stop in front of the store and peer in the window.

"I'm not."

"Yes, you—"

But Ellie's cut off by a woman poking her head out of the door of the salon. "Hello, girls!" she chirps. She has short blond curly hair and she's wearing silver-and-turquoise rings on almost every finger.

Hmm. I'm not sure I'll be getting my hair done here. You can tell a lot about how good a place is at cutting hair from how their employees look. And this woman is in desperate need of . . . I don't know, exactly. Highlights. Or a brush.

"Welcome, girls, welcome!" she says, ushering us inside. "Welcome to the Serene Spa and Wellness Center."

I frown. The sign on the door says HAIRCUTS.

She must notice that we look confused, because she quickly rushes on, "We haven't had time to change our sign yet. We just recently decided to make this into a full-service spa." She throws her hand out in a flourish, like she's indicating how awesome the place is.

Ellie looks at me and raises her eyebrows. I know she's thinking the same thing I'm thinking. That this place definitely doesn't look like a full-service spa. Not that I really know what a full-service spa looks like. I mean, I've only seen them in movies.

But I'm pretty sure they include lots of white towels and well-dressed attendants ready to wait on you hand and foot and bring you whatever you desire, as long as it's good for you. Things like raspberry-flavored sparkling water and cherries dipped in dark chocolate. (Dark chocolate is totally good for you. It has, like, a million antioxidants.)

This place has none of those things. All it has is a reception desk, a few folding chairs scattered around the waiting room, and one nail station right at the back.

"Well," I say slowly. "We don't really need a full-service spa. Um, but maybe we could have a manicure."

"Of course!" the woman says, and leads us over to the nail station. She frowns. "We only have one manicure table," she says. "So one of you will have to wait." She pushes a stray curl off her forehead and smiles. "And the shipment of nail polishes that was supposed to come in yesterday never came, so we're a little limited in our selection."

"That's okay," I say, smiling nervously at Ellie, who doesn't look too happy. In fact, she looks like she wants to hightail it out of here. Ellie's a stickler when it comes to things like customer service. She'll totally leave a place if she feels like she's not getting good treatment.

Usually I agree with her, but how can I leave now? This poor woman seems so excited to have us here. We're probably her first customers ever.

"I want orange nail polish," Ellie says firmly, which is kind of ridiculous, because she doesn't even like the color orange.

"That's wonderful!" Sharon says. "Because that's one of the colors we have."

"Oh, great news," I agree, pushing Ellie toward the uncomfortable-looking chair that's sitting in front of the nail station. "I'll just wait up front and read a magazine or something."

Usually when Ellie and I get our nails done, we sit next to each other and gossip about people at school. But like Sharon said, there's only one nail stand.

"*You're* going to be doing my nails?" Ellie asks Sharon skeptically.

"Yes." Sharon nods and sits down at the nail station. She goes to open a bottle of orange nail polish and almost spills it all over. Yikes. "I just got my nail tech certification a few days ago." She points up to the wall, where a certificate is hanging in a gold frame.

"You've only known how to do nails for *two days*?" Ellie asks.

"Oh, no. I've only been *certified* for two days. But I've practiced on loads of people." Sharon beams.

"Okay, well, see you in a few minutes!" I yell, and then I head back to the waiting area before Ellie can change her mind. I'm sure she'll be fine. I mean, it's just nails. What's the worst that can happen? She gets a little nail polish on her?

We can't just leave and crush poor Sharon's dreams. What if we left and she started thinking she was the worst salon owner ever and that she should just give it up and go back to whatever her job was before? I really don't want that on my shoulders. And I doubt Ellie does either.

I grab a magazine and sit down in one of the folding chairs. I wonder how long it will take Ellie to get her nails done. I hope not that long. The smell of chemicals in this place is starting to give me a headache.

I pull my phone out and check to see if I have a text from Brandon. But there's nothing. I wonder if I should text him. Not that I have a reason to text him, but do I really need a reason? I could just be all casual and ask him about the math homework or something. Of course, he would probably see right through that. I don't want to play hard to get, but at the same time—

"Excuse me," a voice says. "But is this Sharon's Haircuts?"

I look up from my phone to see a girl standing in front of me. She has long wavy dark hair and bright blue eyes. Her skin is pale, and she has a lot of makeup on. Like, a *lot* of makeup—smoky purple eye shadow, bronzer, mascara, and a slick of bubble-gum-pink lip gloss. She's wearing a short black skirt, a hot pink top, patterned tights, and leg warmers.

"Well," I say, "I think that's what it used to be called. But now they've changed the name. They're a full-service spa now." I throw my hand out in a flourish, the same way Sharon did.

"A full-service *spa*?" the girl exclaims. "How the heck is she going to handle that?"

"Who?"

"Sharon."

"Oh!" I brighten. "Do you know her?" Maybe this girl will fill me in on this Sharon person's backstory. Like how she came to own this salon. Maybe there's something really juicy behind it.

"Yes." The girl sighs and flips her hair over her shoulder. "She's my mom."

"Wow," I say, "that's so cool, your mom starting her own salon. Does she give you free manicures and stuff?"

She looks at me like I've asked the most ridiculous question she's ever heard. "Of course not."

Right. Well, maybe her mom's one of those people who want their children to learn the ways of the world and work hard for things. Maybe Sharon was a doctor or something and she's totally rich and sunk her life savings into this place to follow her one true dream. And she doesn't want to spoil her daughter, so she makes her work for everything, even manicures at the salon that she owns.

"Good idea," I say. "It's always better to work for things in life. That's my motto." It's not really my motto, but whatever. It could be.

"Anyway," the girl says, shaking her head and looking at me like I'm crazy. She starts looking around, peering into the back. "What's she doing back there, anyway?"

"She's giving my friend a manicure," I say. And then I realize something. "Hey, are you going to be starting school with us?"

"Starting school with you?" Now she's looking at me like I'm even crazier than before. She's definitely a rich kid. They're always looking at you like you're crazy, even when you're saying something that's totally reasonable.

"Yeah," I say. "You just moved here, right? So you're probably going to be going to my school. What grade are you in?"

"Seventh."

"Me too! Maybe I can show you around."

She shakes her head. "You don't get it, do you?"

Okay, now she's gone a little too far. All I'm trying to do is be nice. Not to mention the fact that poor Ellie is back there with this girl's mom, probably getting orange nail polish splashed all over her.

"Never mind," I say, picking my magazine back up. "Sorry for, like, trying to be nice." Not my wittiest retort, but it should get the job done.

"No." She shakes her head and then bites her lip, looking frustrated. "I'm not . . . I mean, I don't know how this works, exactly."

"How what works? Responding when someone's being nice to you? I'll tell you what you *don't* do—act all snotty."

"No." She shakes her head again. "I'm Lyra."

"Great," I say. "I'm Kendall."

She's looking at me expectantly. Okay, this is getting weird. Like, what is this girl's deal? Why is she out here, in her mom's hair salon, acting like she's never been here and staring at me like she's waiting for me to say something?

"Kendall?" Ellie calls, coming out from the back of the salon. She's holding her hands up. One of her hands has the nails painted orange, and the other hand has the nails painted blue. Which makes no sense.

"What happened to your nails?" I ask her.

"Oh." She looks down. "Um, they ran out of orange nail polish."

Wow. This place is a big disaster.

"Who were you talking to?" Ellie asks. She looks around the waiting area, her eyes sweeping right over the girl standing in front of me.

I'm about to tell Ellie not to be rude (although, let's face it, if Ellie's going to be rude to anyone, it should be Lyra—I mean, she kind of deserves it) when a sick feeling rolls through my stomach.

"Now do you get it?" Lyra asks, crossing her arms over her chest and giving me a satisfied smile.

And then I do get it.

Ellie can't see Lyra.

Because Lyra is dead.

Chapter

2

I know that probably sounds harsh, just coming out and saying that Lyra's dead. But really, it's not. People die. It's just a fact of life. And although it's really sad, it's at least nice to know that they end up in a better place.

And even though Lyra's dead, it's not like she's in any pain or anything. In fact, if you want to feel sorry for someone, you should feel sorry for the people who are left behind. Like her mom, Sharon. It must be horrible for her. So horrible that she's apparently kind of lost her mind and opened a nail salon. Which is why you should always be nice to people when you first come into their places of business. You never really know what's going on in their personal lives.

"I'm not talking to anyone," I say to Ellie now. "I was just freaking out because one of the Jonas Brothers is rumored to be getting married."

Ellie frowns. "One of them already *is* married. And you're not even holding a magazine."

I quickly pick the magazine up from where I dropped it on the floor. "Yes, I am!" I wave it around in the air, the pages flying. Lyra bites her lip, and a worried, sort of skeptical look passes over her face. I can tell what she's thinking. She can't believe that I'm the one who's supposed to help her move on. Well, she doesn't have to worry. I have a 100 percent success rate.

Well. Except for Brandon's mom, Mrs. Dunham. But she doesn't really count. How can she? She has some kind of weird personal connection with me, which I'm sure is against some law of the universe.

"Anyway," Ellie says, sounding exasperated. "Can we get out of here?"

"What about me?" I ask. "Don't I need to get my nails done?"

Ellie shakes her head. "No," she says. "We should just leave. Sharon said my manicure could be free because she ran out of orange polish. And she said you could come back and get one too." She holds out a piece of paper, on which is scrawled *"TWO FREE MANICURES, LOVE SHARON XOXOX."*

"I guess this is supposed to be the voucher," Ellie says, rolling her eyes.

"But . . . ," I start to say. But what excuse do I have to stay here? Yes, it would be nice to hang out at the salon and try to get some information out of Lyra's mom, but how can I really do that without raising suspicion?

"But what?" Ellie asks, sounding impatient.

"Nothing," I say. "Okay, let's go."

We walk out of the salon. And when we do, Lyra follows us.

It turns out that Lyra is actually very good at following. She follows Ellie and me to Poppy's Papeterie and watches quietly as we look through all the journals and monogrammed stationery. She follows us to lunch. She follows us to the chocolate shop and watches us try all the samples while the owner of the place isn't looking. (The owner, Oliver, is not a big fan of us for some reason, which honestly makes no sense. We are such nice girls! And is it really our fault that we never buy anything? The chocolate in that place is so expensive. We don't have jobs. We're only kids. Besides, the country is in a recession. And honestly, if he doesn't want people to eat the samples, then why does he have them out?)

When I finally walk Ellie home and then head toward my house, Lyra's still following me. She lags a few paces behind, not saying anything.

As I round the corner of my street, I can see my dad standing in our driveway. He's wearing jeans and a dark green fleece jacket, and he doesn't look too happy.

"Kendall!" he says when he sees me. "Where have you been?"

"I was out with Ellie," I say. "Didn't you get my note?" I left my dad a note on the counter this morning, letting him know that I was going into town with Ellie. My dad likes to sleep in on weekends, so I'm usually up before him. Which is kind of funny.

"Yes, I got your note," he says. "But don't you remember what today is?"

"Sunday?" I try.

"Today's Sunday?" Lyra asks. She's caught up to me, and now she's standing on the driveway behind me. "Wow." She shakes her head. "It's so weird being dead. You totally lose track of the days." She pushes her glasses up her nose and frowns.

Her glasses say DIOR on the side in tiny letters. She looks very hip and trendy, and I wonder if she really needs those glasses to see, or if she's just wearing them because they're cute.

"Yes, today's Sunday," my dad says. "And do you remember what you were supposed to do on Sunday?"

"My homework?" I try, because that seems like as good an answer as any.

15

"No," my dad says, sounding exasperated. "Apple picking!"

Oh. Right. I totally forgot that I'm supposed to be going to the apple farm today with my dad and his friend Cindy. Well, *supposedly* they're friends—but over the past week or two I've started to suspect that the two of them might be more than that.

Here is a list of the evidence I have procured:

1. Cindy has been after my dad pretty much ever since they met. You can totally tell. I mean, she is always showing up at our house with food. Which is kind of ridiculous. I mean, we know how to cook here. (Well, at least enough to keep ourselves fed.) But Cindy kept bringing over things like cherry pie or chili or fried chicken. And when my dad's doctor put him on a special diet for his high cholesterol, suddenly Cindy just happened to get all into healthy cooking. Her spaghetti and meatballs started getting replaced with grilled chicken and roasted asparagus. So. Totally. Suspicious.

2. She's always complimenting me. Now, you might think that's really nice of her, but if you look below the surface, you'll see that it's a

total ploy to get close to my dad. Cindy knows she needs my approval, so she tries to get it by complimenting my hair and clothes.

3. Cindy and my dad have secrets. Not, like, big secrets or anything. But little secrets. Like, one of them will mention something they did together that I had no idea about. Like, Cindy will be all, "Oh, this reminds me of that bread we ate the other day," and my dad will be all, "Yes, it does." And I'll be like, "Um, what bread?" because I have no idea what they're talking about. Which means they're obviously having some kind of secret rendezvous.

4. My dad invited me to go apple picking with him and Cindy. He came up to my room a few days ago right when I was in the middle of a very important conversation with Ellie, and asked me to get off the phone. I got super-paranoid, because my dad's not really big on talking about emotions or anything like that. So I figured something horrible had happened. But it wasn't anything horrible. It was just my dad asking me to go apple picking with him and Cindy. My dad hates apple picking. But he

was being very insistent, and he was acting all twitchy. Which leads me to believe that today is the day the two of them are going to tell me they're a couple. Which is why when he asked me to go, I promptly forgot about it. Oops.

"Oh," I say innocently. "Is that today?"

"Yes."

"I have a lot of homework."

"You're going."

"Do I have to?" I say. I'm not full-out whining, but I'm close.

"Yes." My dad looks at his watch. "And we're already late."

"Fine," I say. "Just let me change first, okay?"

"You have five minutes."

I run into the house and up the stairs to my room. On the way my phone beeps with a text. Brandon!

Hey—what r u doing today? Wanna hang?

I hesitate. I read this book once that said you should never make weekend plans with a guy after Wednesday. But honestly, I think things have changed. I mean, that book was kind of old, and we're in the information age now. Everyone texts people to hang out at the last minute.

Going apple picking, I text back. I'm in my room now, and I kick off my shoes and open my top dresser drawer. I pull out some skinny jeans and a cute black sweater with sparkly stars on the front. I get dressed, then pull out my soft black boots and slide my feet into them, tucking the bottom of my jeans into the tops of the boots.

I tie my hair back into a ponytail, slick some gloss on my lips, and I'm ready.

Want some company? Brandon texts back.

My heart leaps at the thought of seeing him. And then I think about inviting him. It would be okay, right? I mean, it would only be fair. My dad gets to bring a date. Why should I have to be the third wheel?

My dad and Cindy are going. U still want to come?

I hit send and hold my breath. Brandon and my dad don't exactly have the best relationship. My dad is kind of hard on Brandon. He's very suspicious of him, just because the first time they met, Brandon and I were supposed to be staying after school to study and instead we were at the mall. Which wasn't even Brandon's fault.

A second later my phone beeps.

I'm in—you going now?

I text him to meet us at the corn maze in twenty minutes, then head downstairs with a spring in my step. Apple picking won't be so bad if Brandon's there. And I'm sure my dad won't mind. After all, if he's going to tell me that he and Cindy are an item, what better way to make sure I won't freak out than for me to have a friend there to supervise?

Okay. So I was kind of wrong. And by "kind of" I mean, you know, "completely." My dad is being totally unreasonable about this whole me inviting Brandon thing.

"No," he says, shaking his head as he pulls the car out of the driveway. "Please call him back and tell him that he cannot come."

"Dad," I say as I pull on my seat belt, "I can't call him back and tell him that." Plus I would never call him in the first place. Doesn't my dad know that all important details are relayed by texts these days? He's always going on and on about how many texts I send every month. You'd think he'd have internalized this information.

"Why not?"

"Because that's rude."

"And you don't think it's rude that you invited him along without even asking me?"

Hmm. Good point. "Okay," I say, sighing. "You're right. I'm sorry. I'll text him and tell him he can't come."

"Invite him over for dinner tomorrow night," my dad says. "And give him my apologies."

"Maybe," I say vaguely. I will give him my dad's apologies. I send a text, but there's no way I'm going to invite Brandon over for dinner tomorrow night. Talk about setting myself up for a disaster.

When we get to the apple farm, it's a total mob scene, and we have to wait, like, fifteen minutes before we can even get a parking spot. The place is packed—children with their parents, older couples in flannel shirts, young couples eating apple cider doughnuts. Yum. At least the food here is good.

When we finally get a spot, I leap out of the car and right into a mud puddle. Oops. I hope it's not a sign for how the rest of the day is going to go.

My dad and I walk toward the corn maze, which is where he's arranged for us to meet Cindy. I start to feel a little better as we walk. I mean, what do I really have to be upset about? I like apple picking. Well, maybe not the actual picking, but I like the eating of the apples. And the doughnuts.

And if my dad is going to tell me that he's now dating Cindy, who am I to tell him that he's wrong? I mean, it's pretty hypocritical of me to judge who he's dating when I don't want him to do the same to me. In fact, maybe I can use this to my advantage. If I don't give him a hard time about who he's dating, then he's not allowed to give me a hard time about who I'm dating.

The air smells like falling leaves, and I take a deep breath. It's one of those perfect days where the air is warm enough so that you don't have to wear a jacket, but cool enough so that it still feels like fall.

My boots crunch through the leaves as we walk toward the maze.

"There she is," my dad says, pointing toward Cindy.

She's standing outside the maze, wearing a cranberry-colored sweater and a pair of jeans.

I raise my hand to wave, and when I do, Cindy waves back. And so does the person standing next to her.

And then I realize why. It's Brandon.

"Oh," I say. "There's Brandon!"

"I thought you told him not to come," my dad says.

"I did!" I run toward him. "Hi," I say breathlessly.

"Hi." He looks down at the ground sheepishly. He's wearing a pair of jeans and a white T-shirt under a gray zip-up hoodie. His hair flops over his forehead. "Sorry," he says, holding up his phone. "I didn't get your text until just now. I was already here."

"That's okay," Cindy says, giving us a big smile. "I told him your dad wouldn't mind."

I can tell by my dad's face that he's disappointed. But what can he really do? Is he going to make poor Brandon go home? That would be way too mean.

"Great!" I say brightly. I shoot Cindy a grateful look, because, let's face it, she's being pretty cool about this whole thing. Actually, now that I think about it, Cindy's been pretty cool about a lot of things having to do with Brandon. She was the one who told my dad I should be able to go on my very first date with him, even though my dad didn't really want me to.

I wonder if that means Cindy's boy crazy. I mean, look

at the way she zoned in on my dad. Of course, being boy crazy usually means you're crazy about any boy who crosses your path. And Cindy seems like she's a one-man woman.

"So!" I say happily. "What should we do first?"

Cindy holds up some empty bags. "I bought a couple of bags while I was waiting," she says. "Maybe we can start by picking some Red Delicious. Those are my favorite."

My dad beams at her, like she's just announced we're going to be spending the afternoon flying off to Paris on a private jet instead of picking apples in suburban Connecticut.

"Or," I try, "we could go into the corn maze. And then we could have a hayride."

"Oh, there will be plenty of time for that later," my dad says. He turns around and starts walking toward the apple trees.

I sigh. Everyone knows that the actual picking of the apples is the worst part of apple picking. The ground is always muddy and gross, and no matter what time you go picking, someone has always gotten there before you and picked all the good apples.

But what can I do?

Brandon and I start following my dad and Cindy. As we walk through the rows of trees, Brandon reaches out and grabs my hand. Hmm. Maybe this apple-picking thing isn't so bad after all.

23

For the next hour we pick apples. Actually, my dad and Cindy pick apples. Brandon and I fill our bag up in about ten minutes and then trail after the two adults, walking slowly, holding hands, and chatting about people at school.

When we've finally completed the loop back up to the front of the orchard, my dad and Cindy stand under a tree, their heads huddled together, talking. I watch them nervously. They're probably talking about me. I hope they're aborting their plan to let me know they're a couple.

"Hey," I say, "anyone want to get some apple cider doughnuts?"

"Oh, I don't know," Cindy says. "Should your father really be eating things like that?"

"He can have half of one," I say. "Come on. Let's go wait in line."

We all traipse over to the snack bar. The line for doughnuts is so long that I have to stand on my tiptoes to see over it. But that's not going to deter me from getting the doughnuts. They're that good.

"This place has the best doughnuts," I tell Brandon. "Especially the ones with the cinnamon and sugar."

"I love apple doughnuts," Brandon says.

"Me too."

He leans in close to me then, so close that I can smell his shampoo. My heart hammers in my chest and I feel my face get warm.

"You look really pretty today," he whispers, and a million butterflies swarm around in my stomach.

"Thanks," I say.

In front of us I see my dad reach out and grab Cindy's hand. I feel my breath catch in my chest. I've never seen him hold her hand before. And even though I've suspected they were together, something about him holding her hand makes me uncomfortable.

"Hey," I say to Brandon suddenly. "Do you want to go through the corn maze with me?"

He frowns. "The corn maze? I thought you wanted to get doughnuts."

"Oh, my dad and Cindy can get the doughnuts for us." I grab his hand and pull him out of line, yelling over my shoulder at my dad and Cindy as I go, telling them to get us some doughnuts and that we'll meet them back here in a little while.

"Hey, slow down," Brandon says as I yank him through the crowd. He's looking at me like I'm crazy. Honestly, I probably shouldn't have startled him like that. I mean, he already thinks I'm a little nuts. (There was this totally scandalous thing that happened involving this ghost named Daniella, where Brandon kept finding me in different places, doing weird things—like talking to myself. Or digging up the cemetery. It's too complicated to get into, but I'm sure it didn't make the best impression.)

When we finally get to the corn maze, I'm able to relax a little.

"Have you ever gone through this maze before?" I ask as we wait in line to get in. Luckily, this line is moving a lot faster than the one for doughnuts.

"Nope." Brandon shakes his head and gives me a grin. "Is it scary?"

"Not really," I say. "There's no way to get lost. I mean, they let little kids in, you know?"

When we get to the front of the line, Brandon hands the girl working there four dollars—two for my admission and two for his.

I fumble around in my pocket for my money, but Brandon stops me. "I got it."

"You sure?"

He nods, and I flush with pleasure. So what if Brandon hasn't totally said that I'm his girlfriend? He *obviously* thinks this is a date. Otherwise he wouldn't be paying for me to go into the corn maze with him.

We walk into the maze, and I inhale the scent of corn and hay. There's a slight chill in the air, and I shiver for a second and then turn my face to the sun, letting it warm my skin. Brandon and I begin making our way through the huge cornstalks, laughing and debating which way to go. They space you out so that there's actually not that many people in here with us, which makes it more fun.

We twist and turn and take the wrong way on purpose just to make it more interesting. We get into a playful hay fight at one point, chasing each other around and throwing hay in the air and at each other. It's the most fun I've had in a while.

At one point Brandon chases me into a dead end, and he's about to throw a handful of hay at me when suddenly he drops the hay. "Why'd you stop?" I tease. "Are you scared or something?"

I pick up some hay and get ready to throw it at him, but before I know what's happening, Brandon moves close and brushes his lips quickly against mine. "Sorry," he says sheepishly, looking down at the ground.

Electricity flies through my body. Even though Brandon and I have kissed a couple of times before, it's still a new feeling for me.

I'm not sure exactly what I'm supposed to do. "Oh," I say. My lips feel warm. What do I say? *Thank you?* This kissing stuff is so confusing!

And then I do the last thing you should probably do right after a boy has kissed you.

I scream.

Chapter

3

I don't scream because of the kiss. The kiss was amazing, obvi.

I scream because at that moment the ghost of Brandon's *mom* decides to appear in the corn maze. Actually, she doesn't even really appear. She just peers around the corner of one of the cornstalks. It's very rude, when you think about it. I mean, she knows she's a ghost. Shouldn't she at least try to be a little, you know, respectful?

Of course, it makes sense when you think about it. I mean, she hates me. So of course she's going to want to scare me.

"Ahhh!" I scream as soon as I see her glaring at me.

"What?" Brandon takes a step back. "What's wrong?"

"Oh," I say. "Um, nothing." I try to come up with a suitable explanation for why I would just suddenly start screaming. "I think I stepped on some hay."

"You stepped on some hay?"

"Yeah. I think a piece of it went through my shoe." I hold up my right foot and pretend to be studying the bottom of my boot.

"A piece of hay poked through your shoe?" Brandon sits down on one of the hay bales and pats the spot next to him. "Here," he says. "Sit down. Let me take a look."

"Um, no, that's okay," I say. "It wasn't some hay after all. I just . . . I think I stepped on a rock or something."

"A rock?"

"Yeah, and twisted my ankle." God, I really should have used that in the first place. Stepping on a rock and twisting your ankle is totally believable. It happens to people all the time. A piece of hay poking through your shoe and spearing you in the foot? So not a good excuse! It doesn't even make sense.

"Can you walk?" Brandon asks.

"Oh, yeah, I'm fine." I jump up and down to show him. Mrs. Dunham is still floating around over by one of the cornstalks, her long hair flowing out behind her. She's giving me a death glare. (A death glare, ha-ha. Get it?)

"Come on," I say to Brandon, taking his hand and starting to lead him through the maze. I need to get away from

29

that ghost. Of course, she can still follow me if she wants, but at least we won't be stuck in an enclosed space.

"Where are we going?" Brandon asks.

"We're getting out of this maze."

"We are?"

"Yes!"

I rush him through the maze, following all the twists and turns perfectly until we get out into the open air of the apple farm. I glance behind me to see if Mrs. Dunham has followed us. But she hasn't.

Still. I'm not going to be fooled. She's definitely not done with me.

"That was fun," I say to Brandon. "Wasn't it?"

"Yeah, I guess," Brandon says. He's looking a little confused. Okay, a lot confused. And a little upset. Ohmigod. Does he think I'm acting weird because of the kiss?

But before I can figure out what to do, Cindy and my dad come walking toward us across the apple farm. They're each holding a white paper bag.

"Here you go," my dad says cheerfully, handing one to me. "We got some doughnuts for you."

The bag is warm on the bottom, and when I open it, the scent of sugared cinnamon wafts through the air. Yum. I reach in and pull out a doughnut, then hand it to Brandon.

"So, what do you guys want to do now?" I ask, taking another doughnut out of the bag and taking a big bite. Now

30

that Mrs. Dunham has popped up and Brandon thinks I'm acting crazy, I'm kind of glad to see my dad and Cindy. Hopefully, they'll add some, um, stability to this trip.

"I don't know," Cindy says. Her tone is a little clipped. She crosses her arms over her chest and looks at my dad. "Bob, what do you want to do now?"

But she doesn't say it like, *Oh, what a fun day we're having. What do you think we should do?* She says it like, *You big jerk, Bob, why don't you tell us what we're going to do next?*

Brandon and I exchange a look. I wonder if my dad and Cindy are fighting. What could they possibly be fighting about? All they were doing was standing in line, waiting for doughnuts.

"We could go on a hayride," I try. Hayrides are kind of lame. But maybe it will get them out of their funk. I take another bite of my doughnut. So. Good. How can anyone be fighting when these doughnuts are so delicious?

"I don't think so," Cindy says. "I think I just want to go home."

"Cindy—" my dad starts.

But Cindy holds up her hand, stopping him. "Bob," she says. "Don't. We can talk about this later." And then she mumbles something that sounds like "Since apparently we're not allowed to talk about anything in front of the children."

31

Wow. This is getting bad. Cindy's really mad. (And why is she calling me a child? I'm not a child. I've kissed a boy, for God's sake. Not that Cindy knows this. I mean, can you imagine? That would be humiliating.)

Cindy starts to walk away, and Brandon and I exchange another glance. How awkward. I'm just about to call after her and tell her not to go when my dad beats me to it.

"Wait!" he yells. His voice is so loud that a couple of other people at the orchard turn around and look at him. Wow. He's actually kind of creating a scene, if you want to know the truth. "Cindy, please, don't go."

She turns around, but you can tell she's still mad. I take another bite of my doughnut.

"Cindy, please," my dad says.

"Bob, let's talk about this later," she says. "I don't want to make a scene."

They're already kind of making a scene. An apple orchard is a family place. It's definitely not the type of venue where you should be having a big fight with someone.

"We should all just go on a hayride," I try. "Don't you want to go on a hayride, Brandon?"

"Oh, yeah, a hayride would be fun," he lies. I shoot him a grateful smile.

"No." My dad shakes his head. "Kendall, I have to tell you something."

Oh, God. Here it comes. My dad is going to tell me that

he and Cindy are, like, an item. Or whatever it is you call it when old people are dating. And he's going to do it right here, in front of everyone. "Dad, I really don't think that right now is the, um, right time for this."

"No." My dad's voice is quiet now, and he shakes his head. "This is the exact right time for it." He turns and looks at me. "Kendall," he says, "Cindy and I have decided to take our relationship to the next level."

Shocker. "Oh," I say, "how nice for you both." Honestly, I don't think it's really that nice, but whatever. If my dad's happy, I'm happy. And besides, a crowd is starting to form around us. I smile, in what I hope is a reassuring way, at a man who's ushering his little boys away from us, like he's afraid we're crazy or something. "Now maybe we should—"

"I hope you'll be able to support us as we start this new chapter in our lives," my dad says.

"Of course I will," I say, trying to look shocked that he would think otherwise. We can talk about this later. At home. Away from Brandon, and the random people at the apple orchard. Although, like I said, I'm really not even that worked up about it. In a way it's actually better if my dad and Cindy start dating. Because then they'll eventually break up, the way every couple does.

Except then my dad does something that's so totally unexpected that I almost faint. He drops down to one knee, not even caring that he's getting mud all over his jeans. And then he reaches into his pocket.

"Oh my God," Brandon says next to me.

"What?" I ask, confused. Why is my dad getting down on one knee? Is he really going to beg for Cindy's forgiveness? That's a bit much, especially in front of all these people. I really don't think that a small fight really warrants a big display like that.

"What's he doing?" I whisper. I look down and see that I'm clutching Brandon's arm. But Brandon doesn't answer me. "Brandon," I say desperately. "Brandon, why is my dad down on one knee like that?"

But Brandon still doesn't say anything. It really is like a scene from a movie where something horrible is happening but no one wants to tell the heroine, because they know she's going to flip out.

And then my dad pulls out the ring box.

"Is that a ring?" I ask Brandon.

He still stays quiet.

"Brandon!" I yell. "Answer me!"

"Yes," Brandon says. "I'm pretty sure it's a ring."

My dad holds the box out in front of him and opens it. The crowd gasps. Which is a good thing, because I gasp too, and the fact that they're all gasping drowns out my gasp. Actually, I'm not really sure if I even gasped. I might have screamed a little bit. Or, like, shrieked.

"Is it an engagement ring?" I ask Brandon. Even though the answer is pretty obvious.

"Well . . . ," Brandon says, apparently not wanting to break the news to me.

"Now, this isn't an engagement ring," my dad says to Cindy.

I let out a sigh of relief. It's not an engagement ring. Phew. Dodged a bullet on that one. I loosen my grip on Brandon's arm.

"It's a promise ring," my dad continues.

My grip tightens back up.

"It's a promise that I'm committed to you, and that I want to share a future with you."

"Share a future with you"? My stomach turns, and for a second I'm almost positive I can feel my apple doughnut rising in my throat.

"Cindy," my dad says, staring at her solemnly. "Will you accept this ring, and a promise of a future together?"

The crowd goes quiet. The only thing I can hear is the beating of my own heart in my chest.

For a moment I think maybe Cindy's going to say no. She's just standing there, looking down at the ring in shock. Or maybe confusion. I'll bet confusion. I mean, honestly, who gets someone a promise ring? It's kind of ridiculous, if you ask me. And I'll bet she's going to tell my dad that too. Guys are so clueless sometimes. It's like when—

"Yes!" Cindy says, breaking into a big smile. "Yes, I will accept your promise of a future together."

Cindy holds out her hand.

My dad slips the ring onto her finger.

He stands up.

They embrace.

And the crowd goes wild.

First of all, I would just like to say that I am not one of those people who harbor some secret hope that their parents are going to get back together. I know that's ridiculous for a few reasons.

The main one is that my mom left when I was a baby. She's gone. I haven't heard from her in years and years. I don't know the reasons why she left. I suppose it's because she fell out of love with my dad, but I don't know why she left *me*. Maybe she fell out of love with me, too? That explanation doesn't make too much sense, though, because honestly, how can you fall out of love with a baby?

Anyway, my dad and I don't talk about my mom that much. I think it's too painful for him. And any questions I have aren't really worth bringing up, because they're not important enough to risk making him upset.

One time, when I first learned how to use the internet, I googled her. I found a listing for someone with her name and birth date living in Camden, which is a town two hours away.

I never told my dad I did that. And I never googled her again. What would have been the point? It's actually totally useless to know something about someone if they don't want to see you.

So it's not that I don't want my dad to be dating Cindy because I think he's going to end up back with my mom. In fact, I think it would serve my mom right if my dad went off with Cindy and started some big serious relationship. (Not that I think my mom would even care. Obviously, she left us, so how much is she really going to get upset if my dad's with someone else? Not to mention, how would she even know in the first place?)

The real reason I think I don't want my dad to be with Cindy is because I don't want things to change. I'm happy with the way things are. My dad and I take care of each other.

He makes sure I do my homework and that I have clean clothes and that I'm brushing my teeth and all the other stuff parents are supposed to do. And I make sure he's not eating things that are bad for his cholesterol.

And now he and Cindy are going to be together, and everything's going to change. I mean, think about all the different questions that need to be answered. Will they get married? Is she going to move in with us? Are we going to move in with her? Are they going to have a *baby* someday?

These are the questions that are running through my

mind as my dad and I walk to the car. I think my dad kind of knew I was stunned after that ridiculous scene.

I mean, pretty much as soon as it was over, he led me off to the car, even though a bunch of people in the crowd were still clapping. There was no talk of hayrides or more apple picking, or anything like that.

"Don't worry," Brandon whispered into my ear right before my dad led me away. "I'll call my dad to come and pick me up." He kissed me on the cheek right in front of my dad and everything. Then he squeezed my hand. "I'll call you later."

I didn't even have time to appreciate how sweet he was being, because I was too shocked to really comprehend what was happening.

When I get into the car with my dad, everything is suddenly very awkward. After that whole scene back there, Cindy hurried off to her own car, which was weird too.

I mean, why did she have to scurry away? Shouldn't she and my dad be running off to have some kind of celebratory meal or something to cement their commitment? Obviously, the reason they're not doing that is because of me. Which actually makes me feel awful.

Well, 50 percent of me feels awful. The other 50 percent is angry my dad would do something like that just out of the blue. I mean, he couldn't have come to me and told me he and Cindy were dating? He had to announce it in front of the whole apple farm? And then I feel guilty for feeling that, and just . . . ugh. All my emotions are mixing around inside me like an out-of-control tornado.

For the first half of the drive to our house, my dad and I are silent.

I'm not going to be the one to talk first, I decide. My dad is the one who made this big mess. He can be the one to fix it. I won't speak to him. And if he doesn't start the conversation, I'll just stay quiet. I won't talk to him at all.

I don't care if it takes the rest of the day. Or the week. Or the month. I'll be quiet for a whole year if I have to. People do these kinds of silent protests all the time, don't they? Of course, they're usually protesting something like world hunger or genocide or something. But still.

To distract myself from not talking, I think of all the times I should have realized something was going on between those two. Like the time Cindy mentioned how my dad loves grape jelly, when I'd never heard him mention it in front of her. Or the time I came back from spending the weekend at Ellie's and my dad was all tan and rested, and he told me he'd gone to the beach by himself. Or the way Cindy would always know what kind of music my dad liked to listen to, or what shows he liked to watch on TV.

I look out the window and watch the trees go by, thinking about what it will be like when Cindy moves in and I'm not talking to anyone. Probably it will be very silent.

"So," my dad says finally, shifting on his seat. "Do you want to talk about what just happened?"

I don't say anything. Maybe I'll just be silent anyway, even though he was the first one to talk.

"I can imagine that you're probably very angry," he says.

Of course I'm angry! I feel like screaming at him. But I don't. Because obviously that would defeat the point of being silent.

But then I can't take it anymore.

"Of course I'm angry!" I yell. "Why wouldn't I be?"

He nods, then glances at me out of the corner of his eye. He looks concerned. I don't want him to look concerned. I want him to be wary of me, like maybe I'm about to freak out and maybe not talk to him for months.

"That's fair." He sighs. "I don't think I've handled this the right way."

"Definitely not," I say. Tears well up in my eyes.

We're pulling onto our street now, and I roll the window down a little bit and let the brisk autumn air into the car. It blows against my face, and when hot tears spill down my cheeks, the air cools them immediately.

I keep my face turned toward the window, not really wanting to hear what my dad's going to say.

When we pull into the driveway, he cuts the engine but doesn't get out of the car.

"Do you want to go inside and talk?" he asks.

I don't say anything. I don't care if I'm being a baby. Why should I talk to him after the way he's been keeping things from me? He didn't want to talk to me before all this, so maybe now *I* don't want to talk to *him*.

"Okay," he says. "I just want you to know that I love you very much, and I never meant to hurt you. I'm here to talk whenever you're ready."

He waits another moment, like maybe he's waiting for me to change my mind. Which I'm not going to do.

Then, finally, he gets out of the car.

"Wow," a voice behind me says. I jump and turn around. The ghost from this morning is there. The girl ghost. Lyra. "That was completely ridiculous." She tilts her head. "But I wouldn't worry about it. They'll probably break up, anyway. They're obviously having issues if your dad felt it necessary to do something so over the top. So you probably won't have to worry about good old Cindy being around for too long."

"You were spying on me that whole time?" I ask.

"Not spying," she says. "'Spying' makes it sound like I was trying to do it without you knowing I was there." She moves up into the front seat and slides into the driver's side. She shakes her head sadly. "I can't believe I'm never going to be old enough to get my license."

"You *were* spying on me," I say, opening the car door. If she's so upset about not being able to drive, let her stay in the car and think about it. I know that's a mean thought, but I'm cranky.

"No, I wasn't," she insists. "I was there the whole time. It's not my fault you didn't see me."

"You were there the *whole time*?" What whole time? Just the car ride? Or was she there when I was in the maze with Brandon?

"The whole time," she says, and then grins. "Your boyfriend's really cute."

I can't help but be pleased. Brandon *is* really cute. And it's nice of her to notice. But then my bad mood overtakes me again. She really shouldn't have been spying on me. Not to mention the fact that my dad is making a huge commitment to someone that he just conveniently forgot to tell me he was dating.

"Whatever," I say. "I'm going inside now."

She nods. "Okay, sounds good." She makes a move like she's going to follow me, but I stop her. "I would appreciate it if you didn't follow me."

She frowns. "But then what am I supposed to do?"

"I dunno." I step out of the car and slam the door behind me. She floats through the car and appears on the sidewalk. "Go visit your mom or something."

"I can't go visit my mom!" she says. "Do you know how upsetting that is? All she does is sit in the storeroom of her salon and cry."

I frown. "Why is she crying?"

"Because." She shrugs. "She misses me. And she can't pay the bills on the salon."

"Oh." Wow. Suddenly I feel a tiny bit selfish. I mean, talk about being a spoiled brat. Here I am, getting all upset about my dad being with a woman who's actually been perfectly nice to me, when there are people in this world with real problems. Like bills they can't pay and loved ones who've died.

"Okay." I sigh and rub my temples. My head hurts a little bit from crying. "I'm going to help you to move on." Maybe helping her will get my mind off this whole relationship thing with my dad.

"Move on?" She frowns.

"Yeah. But first I'm going to need some more information. So let me go grab my notebook. And then I'm taking you to the cemetery."

Chapter

4

The cemetery across the street from my house is where I do my best work. I know it sounds creepy, but I think it might be because there are all those bodies around. Just bodies, though—not ghosts. Ghosts don't congregate at the cemetery, despite what all those ridiculous ghost stories will have you believe.

I mean, why would ghosts be at the cemetery? The only reason ghosts are even in this world is because they have unfinished business they need to take care of before they can move on to wherever it is they're going. So why would they spend all their time hanging out at the cemetery? That's not going to help solve their problems.

As soon as I come back outside with my notebook and

my purple sparkly feather pen, Lyra starts in on me.

"Where are we going?" she asks.

"I told you, we're going to the cemetery."

"But why?" She has this totally terrified look on her face, like maybe she's going to be sent into a grave or something. Which makes no sense. She's a ghost. She can move through things. If she got put into a grave, she could just float out of it.

"Relax," I tell her. "It's just where I do my best thinking."

She gives me a skeptical look, and I want to tell her that she's the one who's dead, so she can't really judge me for doing my best thinking at the cemetery. But I don't.

I have to be careful not to take my bad mood out on her. I'm just being cranky because when I went in to get my notebook, my dad didn't even try to stop me or ask me where I was going. I guess he wanted to give me space, but still. He could have at least tried.

When Lyra and I get to the cemetery, I sit down on the bench by my grandmother's grave. My grandma died a few years ago. She was the person closest to me, besides my dad. Actually, I might have been even closer to her than I am to my dad. I say a quick hello to her in my head.

"So what do we do now?" Lyra asks. She sort of hovers on the bench. "Like, what's the exact process for this transformation?"

I stare at her. "Okay," I say, "if we're going to be hanging

45

out for a while, you really need to stop talking like that."

"Like what?"

"Like a scientist."

She beams at me. "You could tell?"

"Tell what?"

"That I want to be a scientist." She frowns. "Or, wanted to be a scientist. I'm not sure if I'm supposed to use the past tense or not." Her hands twist in her lap. "Are there scientists in the place that I'm going?"

"I dunno." I decide this might not be the best time to tell her that she's not dressed like a scientist. Although maybe she's going to be one of those cool scientists who wear couture under their scientist coats.

I open my notebook. On the top of the page I've doodled *"KENDALL + BRANDON"* and drawn a big heart around it. Oops. I quickly flip it so Lyra can't see. Not that she seems to be too interested in my notebook. She's starting to obsess over herself.

"What do you mean, you don't know?" she demands.

"Just what I said." I shrug. "I have no idea where you're going. It's not really any of my business."

She gapes at me. "Not any of your *business*? Aren't you supposed to be a ghost herder or something?"

"I don't herd ghosts." God, what's with this girl? What does she think I am, some kind of shepherd or something?

"Well, whatever," she says. "I'm sure it will be fine." She

takes a couple of deep breaths, like she's trying to calm herself.

"So," I say, "the reason you're here and not, ah, wherever it is you're going to is because you have some kind of unfinished business."

"Unfinished business?"

"Yeah, you know, like a reason you can't move on. You need to fix whatever's holding you back."

"Okay." She shrugs, like this news is totally not a big deal to her.

"Any idea what that might be?" I ask.

She tilts her head and thinks about it. Then she shrugs. "Nope."

"None at all?"

"Nope."

"Any family or friends you can remember having a fight with?"

She shakes her head. "No." She frowns. "I did used to fight a lot with my brother, Micah."

I write that down in my notebook. "What did you guys fight about?"

"Nothing major. It was just normal brother-sister stuff." She looks down at the ground and tries to kick a pebble. But her foot just goes floating through it. "He was actually a really good brother." Her eyes fill with tears, and I stay quiet, letting her have her moment.

"Okay," I say. "So is there anything else you can remember? Anything you think is important for me to know?"

"No." She shakes her head. "I really can't think of anything. Although, honestly, I can't remember a lot about my life. But I have a feeling it was completely normal. At least, uh, you know, before I, uh, died." She frowns. "Wow, that is so weird, to say that I died."

"Do you know how you died?"

"I'm pretty sure it had something to do with my heart. I think I had a bad one." She puts her hand over her chest now, like she's trying to see if her heart is still beating.

"So it looks like we have our work cut out for us, then," I say, sighing. "I'm going to have to do some detective work."

"Okay." She nods. "So what does that mean?"

I shut my notebook. "It means," I say, "that I'm going to have to start spending a lot of time at your mom's salon."

Not that it's that much of a sacrifice. I mean, of all the places to have to spend time, a salon is a pretty cool one. And besides, I'm sure Ellie will go with me. She loves salons.

"No way," Ellie says the next morning, shaking her head as she puts her books in her locker. "I am not going back to that place."

"But, Ellllliee," I whine, "I really need to get my nails done." It's not even a lie. I do need to get my nails done. Of

48

course, I could just do them myself. Ellie and I like getting manicures and stuff, but we're not the kind of girls who need to have their nails professionally done all the time. Like Madison Baker, this girl in my math class. She's always getting her nails done and sighing about how badly she needs a pedicure. It's, like, relax and do it yourself. It takes fifteen minutes.

"Then let's go to that place in the mall," Ellie says. "My mom can drive us." She studies herself in the mirror that's stuck to the back of her locker door. "Do you think this lipstick is too much?"

"No, I like it."

"Are you sure? Because I don't want to look like I'm try-ing too hard."

"Trying too hard at what?"

"Looking good. I want to look effortlessly beautiful."

"You are effortlessly beautiful," I say, wondering how we went from making plans to go to the nail salon to talking about how effortlessly beautiful Ellie is. Not that I mind talking about it. Ellie is very pretty. "You could become even more effortlessly beautiful if you get a facial or some-thing," I try. "We could go after school. My treat." It will cost me my whole allowance, but whatever. It's either that or have Lyra following me around for the rest of my life. The sooner I get started on this the better.

"At the mall?" Ellie brightens.

"No. At Sharon's Spa." Or whatever it's called. Serene Wellness or Sharon's Haircuts or blah, blah, blah.

Ellie looks at me. "Okay," she says suspiciously, slamming her locker door shut and crossing her arms over her chest. "What's this about?"

"What's what about?" I arrange my features into my most innocent look.

"This whole thing about going back to that place." She lowers her voice. "Does this have anything to do with that boy who was there?"

"What boy who was there?"

"That crazy woman's son. Micah or whatever."

"You met him?" My eyes are about to bug out of my head. How did I not know this?

"Yeah," she says. "He was in the back, helping his mom."

"What was he like?"

"I don't know." She shrugs. "He was a normal boy. He looked annoyed that he was spending his Sunday stuck in some nail salon."

I can't believe this! Ellie got to see Lyra's brother. And I didn't.

We're walking down the hall now, and when we get to the door to the English office, we duck inside. Mrs. D'Amico, the head of the English department, lets me and Ellie hang out in here whenever we want. That's because Mrs. D'Amico used to be best friends with my grandma, and she's known me ever since I was a little girl.

"Wait a minute," Ellie says, shutting the door behind us. "So this *is* about the boy at the salon. Don't tell me you like him!" She gets a scandalized look on her face.

"No, I don't like him," I say, rolling my eyes at the absurdity of it. "I like Brandon." I make my way over to the Keurig coffeemaker that's sitting in the corner and start brewing myself a cup of French vanilla. I'm a total caffeine addict. But of course we're not allowed to have coffee at school, so I have to sneak it.

"Okay," Ellie says, sounding relieved. She flops down in one of the big comfy chairs that are against the wall.

I pick up my coffee and then stick another cup under the machine so that Ellie can have a tea. Ellie can't handle too much caffeine. It makes her totally hyper.

"So then why do you want to go back to that salon so bad?" she asks.

"I just think it will be nice to support a local business," I say. "And besides, we don't have to worry about getting a ride. We can just walk there."

I hand Ellie her tea, and she takes a sip. "Does this have anything to do with your dad and Cindy?" she asks gently.

I look at her. "My dad and Cindy? Why would this have anything to do with them?" My stomach twists a little at the mention of them. When I got home last night from the cemetery, I ran right up to my room to finish my homework. At around nine thirty my dad knocked on my door, but I pretended I was sleeping. I just didn't want to deal with him.

"I don't know," Ellie says. But she's looking down at the ground, and her voice sounds all weird.

"Ellie," I say, "what's going on?"

"Okay, fine!" she says, throwing her hand into the air dramatically. "Brandon told Kyle about how your dad gave Cindy a promise ring at the apple farm, and then Kyle told me."

My stomach twists even more. "Oh." So they were all talking about me. I don't like the way that makes me feel. And besides, why would Brandon tell Kyle about my dad and Cindy? He should have known that it was a secret thing that maybe I didn't want everyone knowing about. Especially not Kyle. I don't think Ellie's boyfriend is the type who can keep a big secret. Or any kind of secret, for that matter.

"Is it true?" Ellie asks softly.

I nod.

"Why didn't you tell me?"

"I don't know." I shrug. "It happened so fast, and I guess I just kind of wanted to avoid the whole thing. I haven't even really talked about it with my dad yet."

Ellie nods. "That makes sense."

That's what I love about Ellie. She's always able to see

situations that are complicated and not be, like, *Oh, well, you should have told me, because that's what best friends do.* She's always able to see the reasons why things might have happened the way that they did.

Which is why it doesn't make any sense that I haven't told her about the whole seeing-ghosts thing. I mean, she's my best friend. I don't think she would judge me. But if there's even a 5 percent chance that she might think it's weird or stop talking to me or something, I don't even want to go there. It's just not worth it.

Plus who knows what kind of crazy schemes I would get Ellie involved in if she knew? She'd probably want to help the ghosts move on, and then who knows what would happen? Helping ghosts is not without peril. I mean, just a couple of weeks ago I got into a situation where a girl was this close to getting a restraining order against me. (It was this gymnast at a neighboring high school—don't ask.)

"We don't have to talk about it if you don't want to," Ellie says.

"Thanks," I say. "I really don't want to." And then I do something that I'm not proud of. I avert my eyes and look down at the ground. "I just really wanted to go to Sharon's salon today," I say, "because the one at the mall reminds me of Cindy."

Ellie frowns. "It does?"

"Yes." I consider adding in a sniff and a fake cry, but I'm

actually not that great an actress. Plus that would really be going too far.

"Why?" Ellie asks. She takes another sip of her tea.

"Why what?"

"Why does the salon in the mall remind you of Cindy?"

Hmm. Good question. "Um, because I ran into her there once."

"You did?"

"Yeah."

"You never told me that."

"It was, you know, too, ah, painful to talk about."

"Oh." Ellie's lips scrunch up into a frown.

"Anyway," I say, "I understand if you don't want to go back to Sharon's salon. I know you got a bad manicure there." I hold my breath.

"No, it's okay," Ellie says, her face softening. "I'll go with you. Maybe they'll have gotten better overnight or something."

She reaches out and squeezes my hand.

I give her a big smile.

But inside I feel like an awful person.

Math class.

I'm sitting in my seat, waiting for Brandon to get into the classroom.

My hair is perfectly smooth. I stopped in the bathroom

right before class so that I could make sure it was perfectly soft and falling in a straight curtain down my back. I have a whole technique to achieve this look that involves sticking my head under the hand dryer. I wouldn't have to do that if my dad would just buy me one of those pocket straighteners, but he says I'm not allowed to take hair appliances to school with me. He thinks they're dangerous and a distraction. I bet sticking my head under a hand dryer is more dangerous and more of a distraction. But parents don't understand things like that. They're not logical thinkers.

Anyway, I smoothed my hair because I want to feel very calm. I think it's working. I always feel tenser in math than anywhere else because math is my worst subject. I don't know why, but I don't like the idea that there's only one right answer. Some people might find that comforting, but I just find it scary. How can there only be one right answer for something? It's too much pressure.

I decide that when Brandon gets to class, I will very calmly ask him why he told Kyle about my dad and Cindy.

But Brandon doesn't get there until right before the bell rings. He comes walking slowly into the room as the bell sounds, like he doesn't have a care in the world. If I was cutting it that close, I'd be rushing, my books and bag flying everywhere.

But Brandon is calm and confident. Of course, that could have to do with the fact that he's totally good at math and the teacher, Mr. Jacobi, loves him. Mr. Jacobi doesn't like me. In fact, I think he kind of hates me. I don't know why. I've never even done anything to him. But I think he takes my bad grades as some kind of personal attack or something.

"Hey," Brandon says, giving me a smile as he slides into the seat ahead of me.

"Hi," I say.

"Today we're going to be trying something different," Mr. Jacobi says from the front of the room. He sounds all excited, like this is supposed to be great news, when it actually sounds pretty horrible. Why would I want to try something new? I can hardly get the hang of the stuff we've already been doing. "Today we are going to be working in partners."

I immediately perk up. Partners! Love it! Now Brandon and I can work together, and even have a chance to talk. Obviously, when teachers put you in partners, they don't expect you to actually work. They know it's impossible. They know you're just going to talk. I suspect they do it on days when they're kind of bored with their jobs. That's what I would do if I were them. I mean, math is bad enough without having to teach the same thing over and over again every single year.

Brandon turns around. "Wanna be partners?" he whispers.

"Of course." I blush.

But Mr. Jacobi has other plans. "I will be picking your partners," he says.

This could be bad.

He begins matching us all up. When he gets to me, I hold my breath, hoping he'll put me with Brandon. I think about piping up and telling him that Brandon's been tutoring me in math, and so it would be a good idea for us to work together, but even I know that would be going too far. Plus Mr. Jacobi definitely doesn't like it when I talk in class.

"Kendall," he says, "you'll be with Jason." He turns to Brandon. "And Brandon, you can work with Madison."

What? This isn't bad. It's a disaster.

First of all, Jason Fields is the worst partner ever. He is very good at math. Which you would think would be a good thing, but it really isn't. Jason Fields is actually really mean. One time I had to do a group English project with him, and he went and complained to the teacher that the group was holding him back from fulfilling his true potential. Supposedly he was going to skip, like, two grades, but his parents decided it wouldn't be good for him socially.

And to make matters worse, Brandon's with Madison Baker! Madison Baker is this very popular, very pretty, very spoiled girl. And to add to her list of "verys," she's very flirty.

Sure enough, as I'm gathering up my books to move over to the middle of the room, where Jason is sitting,

Madison appears next to me. She ignores me as she waits for me to move so she can take my seat.

"I like your shirt, Brandon," she says. Then she leans over the desk so that she's so close to him that her arm is almost touching his. "That color looks good on you."

Brandon looks down at his shirt. "Black?"

"I like men in black," she says.

I roll my eyes as I stand up, and Madison slides into my seat without even saying anything to me, or even acknowledging that I'm there.

"Well, I guess I'll go over and sit with Jason now," I try.

"Okay," Brandon says. He stands up and starts turning his desk around so that he's facing Madison. "See you."

Well. Talk about not giving me the good-bye I deserve. Hmmph.

"I already did the assignment," Jason says as soon as I sit down next to him.

"What do you mean, you already did the assignment?"

"I mean that I already did the five problems while I was waiting for you to come over here." He leans back in his chair and raises his eyebrows at me, like he's challenging me to tell him that was wrong.

I want to yell at him, but what can I do? I don't want to admit that I can't do the assignment without his help. And besides, if I try to tell Mr. Jacobi, he'll probably just find a way to make it seem like it was my fault.

So I sit down and try to get to work on the problems. While I do, Jason starts drawing pictures of navy ships in his notebook. His pencil makes loud scratching noises as he goes. It's actually very distracting. When he's done with his picture, he rips the page out of his notebook, shreds it up, and then starts using it to shoot spit wads at our classmates.

Ugh. How gross. You'd think you could expect a higher level of maturity from someone who's so smart, but apparently not.

I try to concentrate on the quadratic formula, entering the different numbers for the variables into my equation. I wish we were allowed to use calculators. It's not really fair to expect us to do our arithmetic with pencils. I mean, how old school.

I'm working on the third problem when Brandon's mom, Mrs. Dunham, shows up. God. She's always popping up at inopportune moments. Like when I'm trying to work on a math assignment.

I try to ignore her and focus on my work, but she starts whispering things into my ear.

"Stay away," she says. "You stay away from him, Kendall Williams."

Wow. This is the first time she's actually come straight out and told me to stay away from Brandon. Usually she just acts all cryptic and scary.

I turn away from her. But she floats over and sits down on my paper. Which is a little weird. I mean, she's a ghost. So technically I can just reach right through her. But how uncomfortable is that? Reaching through the ghost of my boyfriend's mom? Awkward.

"Please move," I whisper to her. "I'm trying to get my education."

Jason Fields stops shooting spit wads. "What?" he says. "Who are you talking to?"

"No one," I say.

"You just said to move," he says.

"No, I didn't."

"Yes, you did."

"No, I didn't."

"Whatever." He shoots a spit wad in my general direction. It lands on my bag.

"That's disgusting," I say, a little bit louder than I intended.

"Is there a problem, Kendall?" Mr. Jacobi asks, looking up from where he's grading papers at his desk.

A few people in the class turn around and look at me. "Um, no," I say quickly. "I was just talking to myself while I tried to figure out this problem."

"Well, try to keep your thoughts to yourself," the teacher says. "There are people in this classroom who are trying to learn."

"Yes, Mr. Jacobi."

I slide my paper a little over to the right, so that it's out from under Mrs. Dunham. But she moves over. So I move my paper. Then she moves more. Then I move more. Then she moves more.

Now my paper is practically off the desk, that's how far she's pushed me. And so the next time she moves, I push my paper again, only this time my math book falls to the floor.

"Ahhh!" I scream. "Watch it!"

I bend down to pick up my book, and when I look up, everyone in the class is staring at me. I mean, like, everyone. And then I realize that Jason Fields has gotten up to sharpen his pencil. Which means that there's no one sitting near me. Which means it seems as if I've just randomly thrown my book on the floor and then just started yelling at no one.

"Miss Williams!" Mr. Jacobi says. "This outburst is unacceptable! Please join me for lunch detention."

"But I didn't do anything!" I protest.

"I'd say that throwing your book on the floor and yelling out during class for no other reason than to start a disruption counts as something, wouldn't you?"

He wouldn't be saying that if he knew there was a ghost here who was messing with me. But what can I really say? Nothing. So instead I just nod.

"She's so weird," I hear Madison Baker say before she turns back toward Brandon.

But that's not the worst part. The worst part is that Brandon doesn't bother to contradict her.

Whatever. Who cares if I have to have lunch detention? Lunch detention isn't as bad as real detention, mostly because you only have to stay for the first fifteen minutes of lunch. And yes, that means that you only get twenty-five minutes to eat, but still. It's not like you have to give up your whole period or anything.

And honestly, I was going to spend my lunch period in the library anyway, looking up information on Mrs. Dunham. She has really crossed the line this time. This is war. If she's going to start freaking out and messing with my academic career, well, then I'm going to have to engage with her. Obviously, ignoring her isn't working.

Of course, the worst part of lunch detention is that I have to sit there in the classroom, alone with Mr. Jacobi. I work on some of my math homework, and he sits there at his desk, grading papers. Every so often he lets out a big sigh and then makes a big red mark through something on someone's paper. Probably mine.

As soon as the hand on the clock clicks over to show that fifteen minutes is up, I bolt out of Mr. Jacobi's room and to the library.

I head to one of the computers along the back wall, then reach into my bag and pull out the ham and cheese sandwich I packed for lunch this morning. I'm not technically supposed to be eating in the library, but who's going to notice me all the way back here?

I sit down, type Mrs. Dunham's name into Google, and scroll through the results. But nothing interesting comes up. Just some stupid 5k races she ran for charity. There's a picture of her smiling into the camera at one of them, with a caption that says *"Julie Dunham raised five thousand dollars for Save the Children."*

That obviously tells me nothing except (a) she liked to run (which just proves she's totally crazy—I mean, who really likes to run? like for fun? only crazy people) and (b) she had everyone fooled into thinking she was some kind of nice person who liked to do things for charity. Ha! I wonder what the organizers of that race would think if they knew what she did to me in math class today. Probably they wouldn't be too happy.

But there's nothing else on the internet about Julie Dunham. She doesn't even have a Facebook page. Of course, she probably died before Facebook was even invented. Sigh. The only real information I can find is that she graduated from our town's high school in 1990. She's listed on the alumni page as Julie Collier (Dunham). Collier must be her maiden name. And then I remember that the school library keeps old yearbooks on a bookshelf by the reference desk.

I head over there and run my fingers over the spines of the yearbooks until I get to the one for 1990. I pull it off the shelf and sit down on the floor, then flip through the pages until I get to Julie Collier. Her senior picture smiles back at me happily. She has big poofy bangs, and she's wearing a gold chain around her neck. Underneath her picture it says *"Most Cheerful."* Hmm. Apparently people change as they get older.

I turn to the index in the back and search for her name, checking to see if she appears anywhere else in the yearbook. There's a whole string of page numbers after her name. I flip through, checking them out one by one. Cheerleader. Yearbook. Foreign Language Club. A bunch of candids—Julie in the cafeteria with her arm around some guy. Julie walking down the hall in her cheerleading skirt. Boring, boring, boring.

But when I get to the next picture, I gasp. I swallow hard, looking down at it carefully. My heart leaps in my chest.

It's a picture of Julie, hanging outside after school.

She still has the same big smile and the same poofy bangs.

Only, in this picture she has her arm around my mom.

Chapter

5

"Come on," Ellie says after school as she pulls me down Main Street toward Sharon's salon. "I thought you were so excited to get a manicure."

"I am," I say, hoping she believes me. The truth is, I'm really not looking forward to going back to the salon. I mean, how am I supposed to concentrate on helping Lyra move on when I haven't been able to concentrate on anything all day? I just keep thinking about that picture of my mom with Mrs. Dunham. Were they friends? Does the fact that Mrs. Dunham wants me to stay away from Brandon have anything to do with my mom? And if so, what?

"Then why are you walking so slow?" Ellie asks. She's a few steps ahead of me now, and she turns around and stops on the sidewalk, waiting for me to catch up.

"I don't know."

"Where were you during lunch, anyway?" Ellie asks. "Everyone was looking for you."

"Really?"

"Yeah."

"Like who?"

Ellie rolls her eyes, like she can't believe how obvious I'm being. "If you want to know if Brandon was asking about you, then just ask me if he was."

"I wasn't wondering about Brandon," I lie. Of course I want to know if Brandon was asking about me.

"So is Brandon your official boyfriend or what?" Lyra asks, scaring me half to death. She's suddenly walking right next to us. Great. The last thing I need is her hanging around while I'm in the salon trying to get information. Actually, it might be good if she's there. Maybe something will spark her memory.

But she should still be quiet until I need her. Especially when it comes to my personal life. I mean, talk about something being none of her business.

"Brandon was asking about you," Ellie says as she opens the door to the salon. "He wanted to know if you had to spend the whole period in lunch detention."

"Oh," I say nonchalantly, stepping past her and into the salon. The chemical scent of nail polish remover hits my nostrils. Wow. That's really strong. Hasn't Sharon ever heard of scented candles? Or at least some flowers or something. The last thing you want to smell when you come into a salon is a bunch of chemicals.

"So you got lunch detention?" Ellie prompts.

"For something so stupid," I say. "I dropped my book on the floor in math, and Mr. Jacobi thought I did it on purpose to disrupt the class."

The salon is completely deserted. There are no other customers, and no sign of any employee waiting to greet us, so I head over to the wall and start looking through the shelf of nail polishes. It seems like they've added a few to their selection. Of course, they only had, like, twenty to begin with, so a few more doesn't really make much difference.

"What color are you going to get?" I ask Ellie. "I think I'm going to get purple."

"I don't think I need a manicure," she says. "I just had one yesterday, remember?" She holds up her hands, waving her orange and blue nails at me.

"Oh, come on," I say. "It will be fun. We can sit together. Look, there are two chairs back there now." I point to the back, where, sure enough, Sharon has set up another nail station.

"Are they even open?" Ellie asks, frowning. "Because there's no one in here."

"They're probably just in the storeroom or something," I say, even though I'm not so sure. I look around for one of those bells you ring when you need service, but I don't see one.

"Doubt it," Lyra says conversationally. "My mom has this weird habit of wandering away and not coming back."

Great. Wandering away and not coming back? That sounds kind of like my mom. Of course, she didn't just wander away. She literally went away and never came back. There was nothing wandery about it.

"Hello?" I yell toward the back of the salon. "Hello, is anyone here?"

"The sign on the door says 'Open,'" Ellie says. "You'd think that if they'd stepped out for a minute, they would have at least locked the door."

Lyra shakes her head like she can't believe how ridiculous the whole thing is. "I can't believe my mom left the cash register unattended. Doesn't she know she could get robbed?"

I want to tell her there's probably not that much money in the cash register to begin with. I mean, honestly, what's a thief going to take? Ten dollars and a few bottles of nail polish?

"Hello?" I try again. "Hello? Is this place open?"

"I guess not," Ellie says happily. "We should probably go."

But I'm not giving up that easily. "Hello! Hello? Is anyone here?" I lean over the counter and raise my voice. From behind the set of double doors in the back wall comes the sound of something rustling. "See?" I say. "They're probably just busy in the back."

"Busy doing what?" Ellie looks around at the empty salon.

"I dunno. Opening shipments of nail polishes or something."

"Yeah, well, hopefully they'll bring them out soon." She gives a pointed look toward the sparse nail polish shelf.

"Ellie!" I say. "Be nice!"

The rustling noise has stopped, but it's soon followed by the sound of a huge crash and a male voice shouting, "Oh, crap!"

Then we hear Sharon say, "Micah, are you okay?"

And then the first voice, which I guess is Micah's, yells back, "I'm okay, Mom." Then the doors to the back come flying open and Micah appears. At least, I assume it's Micah. "Oh!" he says, a big smile appearing on his face when he sees us. "We have customers!"

He sounds half excited and half bewildered, like he can't believe there are actual customers in the store.

"Mom!" he yells. "We have customers!"

"We do?" More rustling, and then Sharon finally emerges. She's wearing a pair of white capri pants and a pink-and-blue-plaid shirt. Her hair is pulled back in a bun, and she has a smear of nail polish on one cheek. When she sees that it's us, her smile falters for a moment, but she recovers quickly. "Ahh! Repeat business. How wonderful."

"My God," Lyra says, looking at her mom. "She looks like a mess." She tries to poke me in the shoulder, but her finger goes right through me. "Tell her if she wants to run a successful business, she's going to have to give off an aura of success at all times. And that includes dressing well."

I'm not telling her that. I'm just a customer.

"Yes, hello," I say. "We'd like to get our nails done, please."

"Wonderful," Sharon says. "Did you notice that we got some new nail polishes in?" She sounds so hopeful and excited.

"Yes, we did," I say. I hold up the purple one I picked. I elbow Ellie, and she sighs and then holds up this really pretty blue-green color. See? Who says you need tons of choices? Everyone knows that people pretty much pick the same ten or so colors anyway.

"Good choices, girls," Sharon says. She tilts her head toward the two nail stations. "Did you notice that we now have the ability to do several manicures at once?"

"Several? Try two," Lyra says, and snorts. She shakes her head like she can't believe how ridiculous her mom is being. She's kind of a brat for a ghost. I'd like to see her try to run a successful business. I'll bet it's not as easy as it looks.

"Yes, we're very excited to be able to sit together while we get our nails done," I say. "Aren't we, Ellie?"

"Thrilled." Ellie looks around. "Where's the other nail technician?"

"What do you mean?" Sharon frowns, confused.

"You said we could both get our nails done at the same time. So you'll do one of us, and who will do the other?"

"Micah," Sharon says, like it should be obvious.

Micah beams.

"Micah?" Ellie's aghast.

"Yes."

"Is Micah certified to do that?" Ellie asks. "Like by some nail tech school or something?"

Micah and Sharon look at each other nervously. I can tell that Micah isn't certified. Obviously. I mean, who in their right mind is going to certify a fourteen-year-old boy to do nails? I don't even think you're allowed in nail school if you're only fourteen.

"Oh, that's okay," I say quickly. "I'm sure Micah knows exactly what he's doing."

"I doubt it," Lyra pipes in helpfully. "One time my mom put him in charge of painting the bathroom, and he made a huge mess."

"Of course he doesn't know what he's doing," Ellie says.

"He's probably never even painted nails before."

"Of course he has," Sharon says. She holds up her hand. "He just did mine."

"Oh, perf," I say, pushing Ellie back toward the chairs. "Your nails look fabulous, Sharon." And they do. At least, from far away they do. And honestly, who's really going to be looking at Ellie's nails up close? Well, I guess Kyle, Ellie's boyfriend, might. But he's definitely not the type to notice things like that. One time Ellie took him to the movies, and he ate popcorn and spilled it all down his shirt and he didn't even care.

"If they look so fabulous," Ellie says to me, "then why don't you let Micah do *your* nails?"

"Because I'm going with Sharon," I say.

"Why?"

Because I want to ask her about her daughter who's a ghost so that I can get information about why she can't move on? "Um, because . . ."

"Exactly," Ellie says. "So you go with Micah."

She pushes me over to the chair where Micah is sitting behind the nail table. He gives me a smile. I feel bad for him. I mean, here he is, just trying to help his mom at her salon, and he's being subjected to ridicule. He probably doesn't even want to be doing nails. He's probably just doing it to be nice. And he's probably perfectly good at it.

"Hi," Micah says.

"Hi." I sigh and sit down.

"Your friend is kind of bossy," Lyra says as she watches Ellie sit down in the other chair. Hmmph. *Takes one to know one,* I feel like saying. But I don't. Besides, Ellie isn't really bossy. She just knows how to take control of a situation. And honestly, if she didn't, who would keep me in line? Without her I'd be all over the place.

"So, this is a nice color," Micah says, picking up the bottle of purple polish. He looks at me for confirmation, like maybe he doesn't really know if it is or not. "It's, ah, pink."

"It's purple," I correct.

"Right. Ah, first I'm going to soak your cuticles," Micah announces. He sets my hand into a yummy-smelling bowl of water. Mmm. The warm water feels good on my skin. Then Micah starts to massage my hand.

Huh. I'm just noticing exactly how cute Micah is. I mean, if you like that type. And by "that type" I mean, you know, good-looking. Because it's not really a matter of opinion. He has floppy blond hair and blue-green eyes and a really nice smile. And he's tall. I think it's very hard to find a tall boy these days. It seems like everyone is a lot shorter than they used to be. Or it could just be that—

The sound of the bell tinkling on the door echoes through the salon.

I hardly notice it, because this hand massage is kind of mesmerizing me, if you want to know the truth. In fact, it feels so good that when Micah finishes and lifts my fingers out of the water, I'm actually kind of disappointed.

"Now, are you happy with the color you chose?" he asks.

"Yes," I say.

"Hello?" a girl's voice comes yelling from the front of the salon. "Hello! Like, is anyone working here or what?"

Then another girl's voice says something that sounds like "God, they don't even have a receptionist. This place is lame."

"Oh, hello!" Sharon yells, jumping up from the nail table next to me. Well, it's not exactly next to me. In fact, it's actually so far away that Ellie and I haven't even really been able to talk. But whatever. Who needs to talk when they're getting their nails done? Ellie and I have enough time to talk at school. And after school. And before school. And anytime she's over at my house.

I glance over my shoulder to see who's come into the salon. I hope it's some older girls with a lot of money who are going to be coming here a lot. Something tells me that Sharon is going to need the business. Of course, if the girls have a lot of money, I doubt they're really going to be coming to Sharon's Haircuts. They're going to go to the salon in the mall. That place has massaging chairs.

But it's not a bunch of high school girls. It's Madison Baker. And her best friend, Katya Rusoff.

Ugh.

"You know that my brother has no idea what he's doing, right?" Lyra asks. She's standing over the nail table, peering down at my hand. "Seriously, he wouldn't know how to do nails if he was the last person on earth."

That doesn't make any sense. Why would the last person on earth need to do someone's nails? If you were the last one on earth, you'd have way more important things to worry about. Like, you know, how you were going to get food.

"Time to start painting your nails," Micah announces. He takes the cap off the bottle of nail polish. But somehow the top slips out of his hand, and as he goes to pick it up, he fumbles the bottle. "Oops," he says, grabbing it right before it tips over. A big smear of purple nail polish goes all over his hand.

"Sorry," he says. Two red spots appear on his cheeks. He's blushing! How cute!

"God, my brother is such a loser," Lyra says, rolling her eyes.

"That's okay," I say to Micah. "Don't worry about it." He's wiping his hand with a tissue, which isn't really doing anything except smearing the nail polish even more. Little bits of tissue stick to his skin.

"Um, you might want to use nail polish remover," I say, pointing to the bottle.

"On my hand?" He looks surprised.

"See?" Lyra says, shaking her head. "He doesn't know what he's doing."

"It's okay to put the remover on your hand," I say. "It will get that right off."

Micah should definitely stick to giving hand massages.

"So, we have some clients here already," I hear Sharon saying to Madison. "So you'll have to wait. But we have a lot of magazines for you to read, and there's some bottled water in that little fridge over there."

"Do you have Perrier?" Madison asks.

"No, but we have Poland Spring," Sharon says.

I turn around just in time to see Madison wrinkle up her nose. Her eyes meet mine over the counter. "Oh," she says, "it's you."

Wow. Talk about being rude. "Hello, Madison," I say, deciding not to stoop to her level, even though if anyone has the right to be rude, it's me, since she was flirting with Brandon earlier today.

"Hello," she says. Then she whispers something to her friend Katya and they giggle.

I look over at Ellie, who gives me a look like *What is that about?* I shrug. But even as I'm doing it, I kind of have a weird feeling in my stomach. Is Madison being so snobby to me because she likes Brandon? But that's impossible. Isn't it? I mean, I've never even seen them talking to each other before today. Of course, I liked Brandon before I had even really talked to him. In fact, I had a big crush on him just from staring at the back of his neck in math class. Brandon has a very attractive neck.

Ellie opens her mouth to say something to Madison, but I shake my head at her. I don't want her to start anything in the middle of the salon.

"Hey, that's that girl from your math class," Lyra says. "I think she likes your boyfriend."

I roll my eyes.

"I'm really sorry," Micah says as he finishes removing the rest of the nail polish from his hand. "I guess I'm just clumsy."

"It's fine," I say. "Really, it's not a big deal."

He gives me an embarrassed smile and then proceeds to start giving me the slowest manicure in the history of manicures. Seriously, every stroke of the nail polish takes forever. I guess he's trying to make sure he does a good job, but it's not really working. My nails are getting a little bit smudgy, even though he's trying to be careful.

Ellie's manicure is done, like, twenty minutes before mine, and she comes over to stand near me, looking over my shoulder while Micah works.

Which doesn't help. I'm supposed to be asking Micah questions about Lyra. I mean, that's the reason I came in here in the first place. I didn't even want my stupid nails done, and I certainly didn't want to run into Madison and have to spend my whole afternoon in this ridiculous salon.

"Be careful," Ellie keeps saying to Micah. Which is actually making him even more nervous. Every five minutes he holds my hand up to show his mom, who's sitting at the other nail station, doing Madison's nails. She tells him he's doing a good job.

"There you go!" he says finally. "All done!"

I haven't even had a chance to ask him one question about his sister. Talk about a wasted trip.

But what can I do? I pay for our manicures, and then there's nothing left to do but leave.

When I get home, my dad is waiting for me in the living room. I texted him to let him know I was going out with Ellie after school, and he texted me back to tell me it was fine. Other than that, we haven't talked since yesterday's scene at the apple farm.

I try to quickly grab a snack from the kitchen and sneak upstairs to my room, but he calls my name when my foot is on the first step.

"Kendall!"

"I'm home, Dad," I say, stepping up onto the second stair. "I'm just going upstairs now to get started on my homework. I have a lot of it, and so—"

"I'd like to talk to you first," he says.

"Can it wait until after dinner?" I ask. Or, like, until never? "I really do have a lot of homework."

"No," he says.

I sigh and then walk back down the stairs.

When I get to the living room, my dad's sitting on the couch, looking all serious.

"Sit down," he says.

I take a seat in the chair across from him. Neither one of us talks for a minute. I'm waiting for him to say something, and I guess he's trying to figure out what it is, exactly, that he's going to say. Although he probably should have planned that out beforehand. Everyone knows that before you have some big emotional conversation, you should decide what you want to say. Otherwise the conversation has the potential to turn into a big mess.

"First, I want to say I'm very sorry for what happened yesterday," my dad says. "Doing what I did in front of everyone like that . . . well, it wasn't right of me. I should have talked to you about it first."

"If it was so wrong, then why'd you do it?" I ask.

He sighs. "Well, Cindy was getting upset with me, because she felt as if I was keeping my relationship with her a secret from you."

"Um, you *were* keeping your relationship with her a secret from me."

"I know."

"So she kind of had every right to be mad." How can my dad be so clueless? I mean, seriously, think about it. He was treating Cindy like some kind of secret girlfriend or something. That's so not cool. I would kill a guy if he did that to me.

"I know," he says. He leans forward, and I can see how torn he is. "She was getting upset with me because we planned to tell you at the apple farm, but then I kind of lost my nerve. Cindy thought I was using Brandon being there as an excuse." He shakes his head. "So we ended up getting into a fight while you two were in the corn maze."

He looks at me like he's waiting for me to forgive him. But he's not getting off that easily.

"So you had to give her a promise ring in front of everyone? You couldn't have just taken me out to dinner and broken the news to me gently?"

He shakes his head. "The promise ring wasn't meant to happen that way."

"It wasn't supposed to happen in front of everyone?"

"No. The promise ring was supposed to be given to Cindy later, in private. Cindy was offered a job in Virginia last week, and she's been thinking about taking it."

"So you were going to give her a promise ring to show her that you were serious about her, even though you hadn't told me that you guys were dating."

He nods.

I cross my arms over my chest. "Why were you so afraid of telling me that you guys were together?"

He thinks about it. "I don't know. I guess I was afraid of your reaction."

"So you decided you'd lie to me instead?"

"I didn't look at it as lying," he says, looking uncomfortable and squirming a little on the couch. "At first I wanted to make sure this thing with Cindy was serious before I went and told you we were dating."

"Why?"

"Because I know how you feel about her."

"And how is that?"

"You don't like her."

"Dad, I didn't like her because it seemed like she thought you guys were, like, an item. And as far as I could tell, you weren't. So I thought she was a little crazy." I remember all the times Cindy was nice to me and I thought she was just doing it so she could get closer to my dad. It turns out she didn't have to be nice to me to get closer to my dad. She already *was* closer to my dad.

"Oh." My dad runs his fingers through his hair and sighs. "I really messed up," he says. "I know that after your mother—"

"Dad," I say quickly, cutting him off. The last thing I want to talk about is my mom, even if avoiding the topic means having to forgive my dad a little faster. "It's okay."

"No, it's not." He leans forward on the couch. My dad's a big guy, six foot two, and he hardly ever shows any emotion. It's weird to see him so upset about this.

I sigh. "Look," I say, "I'm not thrilled about what happened yesterday, obviously. You shouldn't have lied to me. But Cindy makes you happy, so I guess I'm okay with it." It's only a half-truth. I mean, I'm not *completely* okay with it. But I guess I'm as okay with it as you can be when your dad lies to you about dating someone and then gives her a cheesy promise ring in front of you and half the town.

He lets out a sigh of relief. "That's incredibly mature of you, Kendall," he says. "And I really appreciate it. Hopefully, now you and Cindy can get to know each other a little better."

Oh, yeah. Sounds like a real hoot.

"Sure." Not. "But now I really should get to my homework."

I give my dad a hug and then head upstairs to my room.

I lay out all my books on the bed and am just about to get started on my math when Brandon texts.

Hey, what r u doing?

About to start homework, u?

Missing you.

I blush, and am just about to text back that I miss him, too, when Lyra appears.

"Aww," she says, reading the texts over my shoulder. "How adorable." And then she rolls her eyes.

"What are you doing here?" I say, quickly exiting out of the text screen. "Don't you know it's impolite to read over someone's shoulder?"

"Relax," she says, like I'm making a big deal out of nothing. "I wasn't spying on you or anything."

"Oh, really? Then what were you doing?"

"Thinking."

"Good." I nod and then cross the room to my dresser and pick up a bottle of nail polish remover. Obviously, I'm not going to be getting any work done, so I might as well start redoing my nails. Micah made them a complete and utter mess. I scan my nail polishes and pick out a purple so dark, it's almost black. It's not my favorite color, but it looks sophisticated when I wear it with the right outfit.

"That color's way too dark," Lyra says. "You should go for something a little lighter. Like me." She holds out her hand. Her nails are perfectly manicured and polished in a gorgeous baby blue.

"You should have been the one who gives manicures," I say. "Your nails look amazing."

She nods. "I think that's why my mom opened the salon," she says. "I was always into doing my nails."

I raise my eyebrows at her.

"You're surprised?" She's sitting next to me on the bed

83

now, and she leans over and watches as I begin removing the polish from my pinkie.

"Well, yeah," I admit.

"Why?"

"I dunno." I finish with the pinkie nail and go back for more remover. The bottle wobbles a little bit, and I reach down and grab it just before it tips over. Hmm. Maybe I shouldn't have been secretly judging Micah when he knocked over that bottle of nail polish. Of course, he had a much better arrangement than me. He was at an actual table that's set up for people to do nails on. I'm on my bed, using my social studies book as a shelf. Which, come to think of it, definitely isn't the smartest thing to do.

"Because you think I'm a nerd?" Lyra narrows her eyes at me and pushes her glasses up her nose.

"No." I shake my head. "You just seem like you're more into school than fashion."

"I didn't say I was into *fashion*," she says. "I said I was into cosmetics. Fashion constitutes the things you wear." She frowns. "Of course, makeup can be an integral part of someone's look. Especially when—"

"Well, whatever," I say, cutting her off. I'm not really in the mood for a lesson on the history of fashion. If I want to find out about fashion, I'll just watch *Project Runway* like a normal person. Or that other show, *Design Star*. I'm done removing the old polish from my nails, and so I reach for the bottle of nail polish.

"You know, you should make sure you paint the middle of your nail first," Lyra says. "That way, if any of the color bleeds out, it won't go on your skin."

I try it. It works. "Thanks," I say.

"You're welcome." She sighs and then moves away from me so that she's sitting with her back up against the wall. She pulls her knees up toward her chest. "Can we talk about how this works?"

"How what works?"

"Well," she says, "you're supposed to help me move on, right?"

"Right."

"So obviously I have some unfinished business."

"Right." I don't want to be rude, but for someone who's supposedly so smart, she's taking a long time to catch on to this whole thing. It's actually not that complicated. I help her figure out what she still has to take care of, then I help her take care of it, and then she moves on. When you think about it, I'm the one who has to do the hard part. I'm the one who has to do a bunch of detective work for a complete stranger.

All she has to do is sit there and try to figure out what kind of unfinished business she might have. Of course, this can be difficult for ghosts, since they often have a hard time remembering things from when they were alive. But still. Sitting around and waiting for your memories to come back is so not the same as actually having to go out and do things. It's really not fair.

"So what's my unfinished business?" Lyra asks.

"I don't know. You really don't have any idea what it could be?"

She shakes her head and bites her lip.

"Are you sure?" I ask.

She turns her body halfway around so that she's gazing out the window. "I'm sure."

She's lying. I can tell. I've dealt with enough ghosts to know that when they say they have no idea and get a look like that on their face, they usually have at least *some* idea of what might be keeping them here. But usually it's something too painful for them to face.

"You know," I say, picking my hand up and blowing on my nails. "The more you can tell me about what was going on in your life when you died, the quicker you can move on. And trust me, where you're going is much better than just sitting around here all the time."

I don't really know if this is true. I mean, I have no idea where she's about to go. But something tells me it's a good place. Otherwise why would these ghosts have to take care of their unfinished business? Taking care of business seems like the kind of thing you have to do before you move on to somewhere good. Not the kind of thing they make you do before you get sent to a miserable eternity.

"I don't remember anything," she says, still staring out the window. And then, after a few moments, she disappears.

I sigh.

Great.

Looks like I'm going to have my work cut out for me with this one.

Chapter

6

I wake up the next morning in an inexplicably good mood. I mean, honestly, what is there to really be upset about? My dad and I have kind of sort of made up, and even though things aren't completely settled, I feel like they're definitely on the right track. Mrs. Dunham didn't come into my room last night, and anytime she doesn't show up, I consider it a good night. (For a while she was appearing constantly at, like, two in the morning and moving things around in my room. Which just goes to show how totally upset she is, since for a ghost to have that kind of power, they have to have a lot of energy built up inside them. And something tells me her energy definitely isn't the positive kind.)

My dad makes me banana French toast with pecan

maple syrup for breakfast, and even though I know it's probably because he feels guilty, it still tastes delicious. I know that at some point he's going to bring up this whole thing with him and Cindy again, but for right now I decide to just enjoy the carbs.

I'm even wearing one of my favorite outfits—a pair of sparkly shoes with a heel, a tiered black skirt over ribbed tights, and a red sweater with a huge white heart on the front. It's very cute and casual, but still kind of dressy at the same time.

"You look so cute," Ellie says when I get to school. "I love your shoes, and those tights are adorable." Her eyes move up my body, and when she gets to my nails, she frowns. She grabs my hand. "Why are your nails painted a dark purple color?"

"Um, it's supposed to be dramatic," I say, pretending to be looking for something in my bag. "You know, to offset the cheerfulness of my sweater."

"The cheerfulness of your *sweater*?" Ellie repeats.

"Yeah. You know, because it has a heart on it?" I'm still rummaging around in my bag, and then I realize that I'm going to have to actually, you know, get something out of it. So I pull out a pen, like that was what I was looking for the whole time. "There it is!" I exclaim.

"Since when do you have to offset your sweater?" Ellie asks.

"Ellie, don't you know anything about fashion? You always want to pick contrasting colors and, ah, moods." I watched *Project Runway* last night, and they actually did say something kind of like that. Talking with Lyra about fashion put me in the mood to watch that show.

Ellie shakes her head. "Can't you just admit that you got a really bad manicure? And so you had to do your own nails?"

I shake my head. "It wasn't a really bad manicure."

"Then why did you have to paint your nails a different color?" We're walking down the hall now, toward my homeroom.

"I just told you," I say. "To offset the—"

"Save it," she says, holding her hand up. "Even if you were all worried about your contrasting nail colors or whatever it is you're talking about, there's no way you'd take off all your nail polish just because of that. That manicure cost you twenty dollars."

"Ellie," I say, and sigh dramatically, "you can't put a price on fashion."

She opens her mouth to say something else, but I don't have to worry about coming up with another comeback, because Ellie's boyfriend, Kyle, walks up to us then and grabs her around the waist from behind. He picks her up and twirls her around, then sets her gently back down. Ellie giggles and turns around. "Kyle!" she squeals. "Stop it!"

I push down the wave of jealousy that rushes up inside me. Brandon has never picked me up like that in the hallway in front of everyone. What does that mean? Does he not want people to know we're together? *Are* we even together? I wonder if I should just have that talk with him. You know, the one about whether or not he's officially my boyfriend. I know Ellie thinks I should. But really, what would I say? I don't want to come across as being all needy and insecure.

"Hi, Kyle," I say. "What's going on?"

But Kyle doesn't answer. He just gazes past me down the hall.

"Hello!" I say, snapping my fingers in front of his eyes. "Earth to Kyle! I said hello."

He purses his lips and ignores me.

"What's with you?" Ellie asks. "Kendall just said hi to you. Now you're supposed to say hi back and then ask her how she's doing." She rolls her eyes at me, like she can't believe how out of touch Kyle is with social norms. Ha. Her and me both.

"Yeah, I heard her," Kyle says. "I'm just choosing not to speak with her at this time."

"Choosing not to speak to me at this time?" I ask. "What the heck is that supposed to mean?"

Kyle picks an imaginary piece of lint off his sweater and then flicks it into the air.

"Kyle!" Ellie says. She moves a step away from him and crosses her arms over her chest. "Kendall's my best friend, and you're not allowed to just be rude to her for no reason."

"I'm not being rude to her," Kyle says.

"Yes, you are," Ellie says.

He tilts his head and thinks about it. "Okay, fine," he says. "I'm being rude to her. But it's not for no reason."

I frown, trying to remember if there's anything I've done that could possibly make Kyle mad at me. Of course, it could be anything. Kyle is a total loose cannon. Maybe I've looked at him wrong. And then I remember something. "Is this about how I wouldn't let you copy my science report?" I ask. "I told you, Kyle. I couldn't even if I wanted to. We all got assigned different topics."

"You asked Kendall if you could copy her science report?" Ellie asks incredulously.

"Just as a joke!" Kyle says. "I didn't actually think she would let me. And besides, that's not why I'm not talking to her."

"Then why aren't you talking to her?" Ellie asks.

"Yeah," I say, "what'd I ever do to you?" I think about maybe bringing up the fact that if it weren't for me, Kyle and Ellie might not even be together. I'm the one who was always encouraging Ellie not to be so hard on him.

"It's not my place to say," Kyle says vaguely.

"Then whose place is it?" I ask.

"It's Brandon's."

"Brandon's!" I say. "What did I do to Brandon?"

"I told you," Kyle says. "You'll have to ask him about it."

I stick my hand back into my bag and start rummaging around for my cell phone. I have to text Brandon. Can he be mad at me for what happened over the weekend at the apple farm? He seemed so understanding about it at the time, but maybe he was just hiding his true feelings.

I pull out my phone and start punching in a text. And then I have an awful thought. What if this has something to do with Mrs. Dunham? What if she somehow got to Brandon and warned him to stay away from me? What if she didn't turn up last night because her work with me was done? What if she acquired some kind of super ghost strength and she was able to break through the ghost-human barrier and tell Brandon to stay away from me?

And of course he would probably do it, because why wouldn't he? If his poor dead mother shows up to give him a message from beyond the grave, of course he's going to listen.

I'm still fumbling around with my phone when Ellie puts her hand on my arm. "Kendall," she says.

"Just a second."

"Kendall, you don't have to text Brandon. He's right down the hall."

"Great," Kyle says, sighing. "And I really wanted to make

93

sure that I avoided any drama this morning. It's definitely not good for me to get all uncentered."

I turn around. Brandon is walking down the hall toward us. He looks adorable, as usual. The only thing that would make him more good-looking would be if he was smiling. But he's not. Not even close. In fact, he looks more like he's scowling.

I turn back around to Ellie. "I'm scared," I say.

She wrinkles her face up into a confused look. "Of talking to Brandon? Don't be crazy. Just figure out what he's upset about, and then work it out."

Ha! I wonder what Ellie would think if she knew that I was seeing Brandon's dead mother, who has pretty much told me to stay away from him. I wonder also what she'd think if she knew my mom had been friends with his mom when they were in high school, and I couldn't even ask my mom about it because I don't talk to my mom.

There's a tap on my shoulder.

I take a deep breath and turn around.

And then I scream.

Because standing right there is Mrs. Dunham.

"Oh," Brandon says, looking startled. "I didn't mean to scare you."

"Girls are so crazy," Kyle mutters from behind me. Then I hear him say, "Ow!" Probably because Ellie elbowed him in the stomach or something.

"No, you didn't scare me," I say. It's not a lie. Brandon's not the one who scared me. It was his mom. Who's still standing next to him, glaring. She really needs a new look, for real. I mean, her face is going to start staying all pinched up like that. Of course, I'm sure she doesn't really care, since I'm the only one who can see her. But if she ever moves on, other ghosts might be able to see her, and she's definitely going to regret the fact that she spent a bunch of time wrinkling up her face at me.

"I need to talk to you," Brandon says. He looks a little . . . serious. Not mad, exactly, which is good. But still. Something is going on.

"Oh, um, okay," I say.

"Somewhere private," he says.

"Okay." I swallow. "Well, we have a few minutes before homeroom. Do you want to go outside to the swings?" Our school used to be an elementary school before everything got redistricted, and so there's still an old swing set outside in the back. No one ever goes back there anymore, so we should have plenty of privacy.

He nods and then turns and starts walking away.

I feel Ellie squeeze my hand briefly before I take a deep breath and then follow Brandon outside.

By the time we get to the swing set, Mrs. Dunham is gone. Normally I would be happy about this, but I can't relax. I feel all jittery, like I'm going to jump out of my skin. Who knows when she's going to just pop up again? Maybe she went away because whatever Brandon's going to tell me would be too emotional for her. Ghosts are very fragile. Whenever things start to get serious, they tend to disappear.

"Who are you looking for?" Brandon asks as he sits down on one of the swings.

"Um, no one," I say, taking the swing next to him. I push off the ground and let my swing move slowly back and forth. The cool morning air brushes against my cheeks and makes me feel better.

We don't say anything for a few seconds.

Finally Brandon says, "So, what'd you do after school yesterday?"

That's what he wants to talk about? "Um, I hung out with Ellie for a while, then went home and did my homework."

"What did you and Ellie do?"

I shrug. "Not much. Just went to get our nails done."

"Yeah?"

"Yup." I look over at him. He's not swinging anymore. He's just sitting there, staring down at the ground.

I stop my swing. "So, what did you want to talk about?"

He takes a deep breath. "Look," he says, "I need to ask you something, and I want you to just be honest with me."

My stomach does a flip. Whenever someone says they need to ask you something and they want you to just be honest with them, something horrible is about to happen. That's because it usually means that whatever they're about to ask you is going to have a very bad answer, *especially* if you're honest about it.

"Okay," I say. I'm clenching the chains of my swing so hard that I'm probably going to have marks on my hands after this. He's definitely going to ask me about his mom. About if I can see her or not. I don't know how, but Mrs. Dunham has somehow gotten him a message from the other side of the grave.

And now Brandon's going to ask me about it, and he's going to tell me that he doesn't know how or why it's happening, but of course he has to take it seriously, and that he's really sorry, but he's going to have to—

"Do you like someone else?" Brandon asks.

I'm so shocked that for a second I don't think I've heard him right. "What?" I say dumbly.

"Do you like someone else?" He looks down at the ground again. The early morning sun glints off his hair, showing the blond highlights he has. It's so not fair that a boy is the one who ends up with natural highlights. I mean, women pay good money to get their hair to look like that.

"No, I don't like anyone else." Why would he think that? Unless . . . "Why, do you like someone else?"

"No." He waits a beat. "Are you sure you don't have anything you want to tell me?"

"No." I shrug.

"Okay." He sighs. "I just. . . I don't want to sound like a jerk, or come across as being some super-jealous freak. It's just that Madison Baker said that you were at the nail salon yesterday with Ellie, and that you were flirting with some guy."

I wrinkle up my nose. "There are no guys at the nail salon, Brandon. Trust me."

"That's what I thought too. But she said he works there. Apparently he's the owner's son or something?"

"Oh," I say, my breath going out of me in one big relieved whoosh. "You mean Micah."

"You know his name?" Brandon frowns.

"Yeah. I mean, he was doing my nails."

"He was doing *your nails*?" Brandon repeats.

This conversation isn't going so well. And I can't figure out why, exactly. I shake my head. "I don't understand what's going on here," I say.

"What's going on is that I don't like when Madison Baker calls me and tells me that some other man is giving you a hand massage."

Whoa. Madison Baker is calling him? And what is he talking about, some other man? Brandon's totally gorgeous, and Micah's in eighth grade, but I wouldn't exactly call either one of them a man. I don't think you can really be a man until you get really old. Like twenty at least.

"How does Madison Baker have your phone number?" I ask. I try to sound nonchalant, but even I can hear the edge that pops into my voice. But I don't really care. If he's going to be all upset about me going to the nail salon, then I can certainly be upset that he's getting calls from other women. I mean, girls.

"I don't know," he says. "I think she got it off the class list." Okay. Well, that's not so bad. At least he didn't give it to her. "But don't try to change the subject."

"What subject?"

"Micah!" He pushes his feet off the ground, and his swing moves back and forth.

"I told you," I say. "He was doing my nails." And then I realize something. "Wait a minute," I say, shaking my head. "I think you've forgotten something very important about this whole conversation."

"What?"

"The fact that you have no right to be angry." It's true. Brandon has never asked me to be his girlfriend. He's never told me we're exclusive. And yes, it's true that we've kissed, and held hands, and that we text every day and sit together at lunch, but still. I don't have a commitment. Even Kyle, who might be the craziest guy at our school, realizes that you need to have a commitment. And so he did the right thing and asked Ellie to be his girlfriend.

I'm beginning to see why Cindy was so mad at my dad.

Guys are clueless when it comes to things like this. I guess it doesn't really matter if you're a boy or a man.

"Don't have a right to be angry?" Brandon asks. "Of course I do. We kissed on Sunday!"

"Yeah, but you've never said that you wanted to be my boyfriend. And besides, if you have a right to be angry about Micah, then I have a right to be angry about Madison calling you."

"I told you, she got my number off the class list. She just called me out of the blue. I didn't recognize the number, so I answered it."

I jump off the swing and turn around to face him. "Well, all I was doing was getting my nails done. And I would like to think that you would trust me a little more than that. And if you don't, well then, I have nothing else to talk to you about, Brandon Dunham."

I start to walk back toward the school, but he calls after me.

"Kendall!"

I take an extra step before I turn around, just to make him nervous. "Yes?"

He gets up off his own swing and comes over to me. He sighs. "Look, I'm sorry."

I cross my arms over my chest and raise my eyebrows at him. I give him a skeptical look and hope that he gets the message. The message being that I'm willing to listen to whatever he has to say, but that he better make it good.

"I just didn't like hearing that you were flirting with someone else," he says. "If I'm being totally honest, I guess I was jealous."

I grin. Brandon Dunham was jealous? Over me? I have to admit that I'm a little bit flattered.

"And you're right when you say that I don't really have a reason to be mad," he says. He looks down at the ground, and the sun glints off his hair again. God, he is so cute. "Because you're not technically my girlfriend."

"You're right," I say. "I'm not." Butterflies are taking off in my stomach, seemingly multiplying as they fly around inside me. I feel an electricity in the air, like something really exciting is about to happen. My heart is beating fast in my chest, and I'm afraid that if Brandon gets any closer, he's going to be able to hear it.

Brandon reaches down and takes both my hands in his. His fingers are warm, and a wonderful little shiver slides through my body. "Kendall," Brandon says, "will you be my girlfriend?"

"Yes," I say. "Yes, I will."

He grins, then leans down and kisses me.

Fireworks explode behind my eyes, and my knees get all weak.

My first boyfriend! I cannot wait to tell Ellie.

Chapter

7

"So how did he say it, exactly?" Ellie asks as we walk home from school. It's kind of a far walk to my house, but today Ellie and I really need to talk. It would have been perfect if Ellie could have just taken my bus home with me, but last year there was a big scandal with this girl running away from home by manipulating the bus pass system. So now you totally have to have a bus pass that's signed by, like, the president or something. It's all very ridiculous and unnecessary.

"He just said 'Kendall, will you be my girlfriend?'"

"And then you said yes?"

"Yes."

"How did you say it?"

I tilt my head and think about it. "Like, kind of happy

but not too eager, you know? I didn't want him to think he was doing me any favors or anything."

Ellie nods, then moves her backpack to her other shoulder. "And then how was the kiss?"

"Good."

"Just good?"

"Great. Amazing, even."

Ellie squeals.

This is why she's my best friend. Who else would go through all these details with me? No one. But Ellie will because she knows that I'm all jazzed up about it and that I really need to talk.

When we get to my house, I invite Ellie in for a snack. I'm hoping my dad isn't home yet. Something tells me he's not going to be too excited to listen to me and Ellie talk about how me and Brandon are finally official.

"We should go on a double date this weekend," Ellie says. "With our *boyfriends*."

I giggle. It sounds so weird, her saying "our boyfriends." But in a good way.

I open the refrigerator and pull out a package of carrot sticks and some hummus. Ellie's a vegetarian, so I like to keep healthy snacks on hand. But she shakes her head.

"Oh, no," she says. "News like this calls for junk food." She gets up and starts going through the cupboards, pulling out anything she can find that's bad for you. By the time she's done, there's a small pile on the table of Cheetos, Oreos, Mike and Ikes, and sour cream and onion chips. She's even managed to find some old Halloween candy.

"I don't think we should eat these," I say, picking up one of the fun-size chocolate bars and giving it a look. "I don't know how long they've been in there. They could be from, like, three Halloweens ago."

Ellie reaches into the refrigerator and pulls out a tube of cookie dough. "First we will make cookies," she declares. "Then we will snack while we wait for them to bake, and then we will eat the cookies."

"Perfect." I reach into the bag of Cheetos and pop one into my mouth.

Ellie pulls out a cookie sheet and starts arranging the dough, making the cookies way bigger than you're supposed to. "We need big cookies," she decides. "And we need them with M&M's in them."

She opens a package of M&M's, and we both start pushing the candies into the cookies, making little designs with them. We're giggling and having a good time when Lyra decides to show up.

Whatever. I'm not going to let a ghost ruin my good time. So really, it's just a matter of ignoring her, la, la, la.

"Kendall!" she cries. It's the first time she's used my name, and it's kind of startling. Also, she's screaming, which isn't really nice. Doesn't she know that you're supposed to use indoor voices when you're, you know, indoors? I turn my back to her and take the sheet of cookies and slide it into the oven.

"Kendall!" she says again.

If she's waiting for me to answer her, she's in for a long wait. I mean, I couldn't talk to her even if I wanted to. Ellie's standing right here.

"Kendall, please," Lyra says. I look over at her. She looks like she's been crying. Wow. Her face is a blotchy red mess, and her hair looks all tousled, like maybe she's been pulling at it or something. "Please, I . . . I just remembered something."

Oh, now she remembers something? Yesterday it was all, "Oh, I don't remember anything" and "I have no idea what you're talking about" and "I guess you're on your own." Now that I'm actually in the middle of a social engagement and having fun talking about having my very first real actual boyfriend, she remembers something. So typical.

Well, it's too bad if she's upset. She's just going to have to wait.

"Those cookies smell delicious," I say to Ellie. Then I pop some M&M's into my mouth. No point letting the extra ones go to waste, right?

"They *are* going to be delicious," Ellie says. She plops down in the chair next to me. "Is your dad going to be mad when he sees all the food we ate?"

I shake my head. "He doesn't care. And even if he did, he wouldn't really be able to say anything. He has a lot of making up to do."

Ellie nods. I finally filled her in last night on the phone about all the drama that went down at the apple farm.

"Kendall!" Lyra screams. "Please, this is serious. I have to tell you something. And it's really important."

Doubtful.

"It really is," she says, like she knows what I'm thinking. "I swear." She tries to pull on my sleeve, but of course her hand just floats through my sweater. Then she bites her lip and looks right at me. "Kendall," she says, "this is important. It has to do with Brandon. And with his mom."

"This better be worth it," I mutter fifteen minutes later as I walk across the street with Lyra. We're going to the cemetery. My dad will be getting home soon, and I knew I would need total privacy if I wanted to be able to have a real conversation with Lyra. It's one thing to be talking about Brandon with Ellie while my dad's around. It's another thing altogether to be talking to a ghost that no one else can see.

"It'll be worth it," Lyra says. "I promise."

I sigh. Once Lyra brought up Brandon, I couldn't just ignore her. Especially if whatever she has to tell me somehow involves Mrs. Dunham.

Of course, I couldn't just leave Ellie in my kitchen, so I had to get her out of there. I made up some stupid excuse about how I had just remembered that my dad was coming home early, and how he didn't want me having friends over. Which was completely ridiculous, since I had just told her that my dad didn't care if she was over and eating snacks with me. But I kind of panicked when Lyra brought up Mrs. Dunham, and I couldn't really focus enough to come up with a suitable lie. I even shut off the oven and left the cookies we were making half baked.

"Okay," I say, sitting down on the bench by my grandma's grave. I open up to a fresh page of the notebook I brought so that I can take some notes. I love notebooks. I know it's old-school, and that I could just make notes in my phone or whatever, but it's nice to actually write things down. Plus notebooks are fun to shop for. I have all kinds of notebooks—notebooks to write down new hairstyles, notebooks to write down ideas for when I grow up and become a famous author, and notebooks where I take notes on what the ghosts tell me so that I don't forget anything when I'm trying to help them.

"Okay, so," Lyra says, taking a big breath. "Last night I was a little bored, you know?"

I nod. I can understand that. I mean, ghosts don't need sleep, and they can't touch anything, so what are they really supposed to do? They can't turn the pages of books, they can't turn computers on . . . they can't even really spy on anyone at night, because everyone is usually sleeping. Although there was this one ghost who used to go watch TV with this guy Dale who lives down the street from me—Dale is always up late because he works nights.

"So," Lyra continues, "I went back to my old house."

"Went back to old house," I write in my notebook. "Your old house that you used to live in?"

"Yes." Lyra nods, and then tugs on her hair. "I just wanted to go back there, you know? Just to see it. But when I got there, it was empty. And everything was all boarded up."

I frown. "Didn't your mom sell it?"

She nods. "Yeah, but I guess maybe the new people haven't moved in yet or something. It looked like there was a bunch of work being done, so maybe the new owners are waiting until it gets finished to move in."

"House empty," I write down. "Okay," I say. "So then what?"

"So then I decided that maybe I'd go and look around at some other houses."

Uh-oh. I can see where this is going. "You went to a boy's house, didn't you?"

She shakes her head, and her eyes get all wide. "No!"

"It's okay to admit it," I say. "I'd probably do the same thing."

"No! I didn't go to a boy's house." She takes a deep breath and readjusts her glasses. "I went to my best friend's house."

"Oh. Well, yeah, that makes sense. I'd do that, too."

"Anyway," she says, "I was there, and I was just sort of wandering around outside her house. Rachel has this really cool tree house in her backyard, and so I floated up there and just hung around for a while, remembering all the good times we had. And then I noticed that her bedroom light was on."

"Okay."

"So I went up to her room."

"And?" God, this girl talks slow. Get to the punch line, already. I doodle a flower in the margin of my notebook.

"And Rachel was lying on top of her bed, crying."

"Oh." I frown. "And you think it was because of you?"

"Well, that's what I thought at first," Lyra says. Her voice is cracking a little as she talks about her friend crying. It's really sad, and I get a lump in my throat. I don't know what I would ever do if I didn't have Ellie. Or my dad.

Suddenly I feel like a complete brat for giving my dad a hard time about Cindy. I mean, he's still here. I still have him. To get upset about something so small is kind of crazy, especially after how good my dad has been to me. It can't have been easy for him to raise a daughter all by himself, and yet I've never heard him complain or get upset about it. Not even once.

"But when I got closer, I could see that Rachel was looking at her phone and reading texts," Lyra says. "Her phone kept beeping with new ones, and every time she'd look at the phone, she'd start crying even harder."

"Wow," I say, scribbling away in my notebook. "So someone is texting her."

Lyra nods.

"So who was it?" I ask.

"Who was what?"

"Who was texting Rachel?"

"Oh," Lyra says, shrugging. "I dunno."

"You don't *know*?"

"How could I?" Lyra says. "After Rachel got a few more texts, she shut her phone off and then put it in her desk drawer." She holds up her hands. "And in case you've forgotten, these hands can't do much with solid objects."

"I didn't forget," I say, rolling my eyes.

Lyra takes a deep breath and then stares out into the cemetery. The sun is starting to move down behind the trees, and the branches throw shadows onto the dirt path that winds through the graves. A breeze kicks up, and the leaves move and rustle.

I give her a second, letting her collect her thoughts before she goes on with her story. I'm dying to know what else she found out—especially the part about Mrs. Dunham—but I know this is difficult for her, and I want to give her a second to regroup.

But after a minute or so, Lyra still hasn't said anything else.

I clear my throat, hoping that maybe the sound will jolt her out of whatever brain fog she's in. But it doesn't. She just continues to sit there, not saying anything.

"Hello?" I say.

"Hi," she says. She swings her legs back and forth under the bench.

"So then what?"

She frowns. "So then what, what?"

"So then what happened?"

"Well, I wasn't going to just stand there watching her cry." She wrinkles up her nose. "That would be creepy and highly inappropriate." I resist the urge to roll my eyes. This from a girl who snuck into her best friend's bedroom late at night. I mean, she's obviously not exactly the best judge when it comes to what's inappropriate and creepy.

"So then what did you do?" I ask patiently.

"I left."

"And then what?" I hold my breath, waiting for her to tell me what happened with Mrs. Dunham. She must have run into her or something on the way back. Ghosts are always more active at night. I'm not really sure why. I mean, it's not like anyone can see them during the day anyway.

"And then I came back to your house."

"And you ran into Mrs. Dunham on the way?"

"Who?"

"Brandon's mom!"

"No, I didn't run into her." She shakes her head. "But I should let you know that she's always in your room at night."

"She is?"

"Yeah." Lyra jumps off the bench and starts pacing. "She just sort of sits there, watching over you. It's very weird."

"Does she look . . . angry?"

"Sort of." Lyra shrugs. "What's the deal with her, anyway? She doesn't like you or what?"

"It's complicated," I say.

"She's probably just super-protective of her son," Lyra says, nodding like she knows all about it.

"Wait a minute," I say, snapping my notebook shut. "Why did you say that you ran into Mrs. Dunham if you didn't?"

"I never said I ran into Mrs. Dunham."

"You said what you had to tell me had something to do with Brandon's mom!"

"Oh." Lyra bites her lip and then looks down at the ground. "Well, I knew that was the only way you would listen to me."

I stare at her, aghast. "So you *lied* to me?"

"Not lied, exactly," she says. "I mean, I did see Mrs. Dunham later in your room. And I was going to tell you about it. So technically what I said wasn't a falsehood."

"Technically what you said wasn't a *falsehood*?" I repeat. "Oh, no way are you getting away with that explanation." I leap up from the bench and start walking back toward my house. I'm mad at her now. And I don't want her to think that I'm going to just forget about it.

"Kendall, please," she says, calling after me. But I keep going.

"I'm sorry," she says, rushing to catch up to me. "I've just been having a really hard time. It was hard seeing Rachel crying like that."

I slow down just a little.

"I don't know how," she says, "but I just feel like those texts have something to do with me. Like it was somehow my fault that she was crying."

Now *Lyra* is crying, and that kind of settles it. I mean, I can't turn my back on someone who's crying. It just wouldn't be right.

I sigh and slow down a little more. "It's okay," I say. "Don't worry about it. We're going to figure it out. We're going to make Rachel stop crying, and we're going to make sure that you move on."

She nods and then wipes her nose. I wish I could give her a hug, but it's not really possible.

"How are you going to do it?" she asks.

"I'm not sure," I say honestly. "Any ideas?"

"My brother Micah was kind of close to Rachel," she says. "Maybe you could find a way to ask him if he has any idea about what's going on with her."

Great. The last person I want to be around looks like he might hold the key to me helping Lyra to move on.

That night I have this super-amazing dream where Brandon and I are having a picnic up on a cloud. It's crazy beautiful. We're just floating along, eating crackers and cheese as we look down at everything below us.

"You're amazing, Kendall," he's saying. "I can't believe how lucky I am to be with you. It would be really horrible if I ever ended up with someone ridiculous like Madison Baker."

I'm nodding and agreeing, and he's just about to lean over and kiss me when I start to hear Mrs. Dunham's voice.

"Get out of my dream," I tell her crankily. But she doesn't listen.

She just keeps saying, "Kendall Williams, leave my son alone. Kendall Williams, leave my son alone."

She keeps chanting it over and over, and when I wake up, I can still hear it in my head, reverberating like some kind of annoying cheer at a football game.

And then I realize why. It's because Mrs. Dunham isn't

chanting in my dream. She's chanting right here, in my room. She's over in the corner and she's looking at me and saying, "Kendall Williams, leave my son alone." Her hair is all crazy and her eyes are all bright, and she looks really agitated.

Honestly, it's pretty creepy.

"Stop it!" I say to her. I can't really yell, because if I do, my dad's going to hear me. I throw a pillow at her, but of course it just flies right through her body. "Go away!"

But she just keeps chanting.

It's getting louder and faster, and I close my eyes and hope that if I ignore her, she'll go away. But the fact that I'm trying to ignore her does nothing except seem to make her angrier. She moves closer to my bed, and she's screaming now.

I march over to the door and flip on the light. I look her right in the eye and cross my arms over my chest.

"Listen," I say, "I like your son. He likes me. I'm not going to do anything bad to him, so get over it. We're probably not even going to get married. We're only in middle school, for God's sake!"

I'm hoping if I show Mrs. Dunham I'm not a pushover, she'll disappear. And I'm also totally willing to be reasonable. I can admit that I might not marry Brandon. (Notice I didn't say *definitely*. It can totally happen. I was watching a wedding show the other night on Bravo, and the couple getting married had been together since they were thirteen. Totes cute!)

But appealing to Mrs. Dunham's logical side doesn't seem like it's working. She balls her hands into fists at her sides, and if she wasn't a ghost, I'd probably be afraid she was going to hit me.

Instead she closes her eyes tight and gets a look of intense concentration on her face.

My pulse speeds up and my stomach starts to do flip-flops. I've never seen a ghost do anything like that before, and it's making me anxious.

"Hey," I say, "what are you doing? Maybe we should just take a time-out and talk. If you got to know me, you might—"

But before I can finish what I'm saying, the lights in my room start to flicker on and off. Mrs. Dunham still has her eyes closed in concentration.

"Hey!" I say. "Stop that!"

But the lights just keep flickering.

"What are you doing?" I demand. "Stop doing that!"

But of course she doesn't listen. The lights are flickering faster and faster now, and I reach over and hit the light switch. But the lights don't go off. They just keep flickering, on and off, on and off, faster and faster until I start to get dizzy.

"Please stop!" I'm yelling now, but I don't even care. I

kind of want my dad to wake up and come in here at this point. Who cares if he thinks I'm crazy?

The sound of something humming fills the air. It's almost electric, like the kind of thing you'd hear if you got too close to an electric fence. It gets louder and louder, until finally there's a loud pop.

And then everything goes dark.

Chapter

8

"It must have been a power surge or something," my dad says that morning as he hands me a granola bar. "I'm not sure what time the power went out, so we probably shouldn't eat anything in the fridge."

"Yeah," I say. "Probably not." I open the granola bar and take a bite, wishing it was French toast, or at least cereal. But of course we can't use the milk. I know exactly what time the power went out—3:12 a.m. But to tell my dad that would be admitting that I know something about it.

Once Mrs. Dunham finished her big show, she disappeared. I crept out of my room and down the hall, to check in on my dad. He was sleeping soundly, although the whole house was dark.

I slid back into my bed and lay awake, listening to my iPod pretty much all night. I was too afraid to go back to sleep. I debated whether or not I should wake up my dad, but I didn't want to deal with all the questions. I was afraid I'd break down and maybe tell him something that would make him think I was crazy.

So I just waited until he woke up at six. He went into the bathroom and tried the light switch, and then I heard him say, "Huh."

I've been pretending like I don't know anything about what happened. Which isn't a total lie. I mean, I don't know *exactly* what Mrs. Dunham did to our electricity. I'm not an electrician. And any information I tell my dad isn't going to help him anyway. I'm sure whoever he hires to come over and fix it isn't going to be like, *Oh, a ghost did this? Why didn't you tell me? It would have saved me a lot of diagnostic work.*

"Well, I'll have to take the morning off from work," my dad says. "Hopefully, we'll be able to get someone to come out and look at it right away."

He's over at the kitchen table now, typing away on his laptop, looking for an electrician to come over and look at things. I chew on my granola bar slowly, thinking about how serious this situation is becoming.

I mean, blowing out the electricity in my house? What if she'd started a fire or something? What could be so bad that Mrs. Dunham is that determined to keep me away from Brandon? And then I remember the picture of her in the yearbook. The one of her with my mom.

Could my mom have anything to do with this? Part of me really doesn't want to know. But the other part of me realizes that it might be time to find out exactly what's going on with Brandon's mom. Up until now I guess I've kind of been avoiding it. Mostly because I'm afraid to find out.

"So, Dad," I say nonchalantly as I take a sip out of the glass of water he set in front of me. "You knew Mom in high school, right?"

He frowns and glances up from his laptop. "Yes," he says. "Although we didn't start dating until later. She was a couple of years behind me."

I nod. "What was she like in school?"

"What was she like?"

"Yeah, you know, did she have a lot of friends?"

"She was popular, yeah," my dad says distractedly. He's still typing away on the computer. Jeez. I mean, I know he really wants to get this whole us-having-no-electricity thing taken care of, but this is the first time I've asked about my mom in, like, years. You'd think that maybe he'd want to pay a little more attention. I'm obviously crying out for help.

"Who was her best friend?" I ask.

"Oh, I don't know," he says vaguely. "She had a lot of friends."

"Really?" I peel the wrapper farther off my granola bar. I take a bite, chew, and then swallow. "Because I was looking at some old yearbook pictures of her, and it seemed like maybe she spent a lot of time with this girl named Julie."

I'm not sure if it's my imagination or not, but I feel like I see a certain look flicker over my dad's face. It's the kind of look you get when someone has brought something up that you really don't want to talk about but you know you can't just *say* you don't want to talk about it, because if you do, the other person will get suspicious.

"Huh," my dad says. "Yeah, Julie. I remember her. Mm-hmm, Julie. She was one of your mother's, ah . . . I mean, yes, they were friends."

Wow. He's getting all stumbly. I take a sip of my water. "Julie Collier, right?"

"Yup, mm-hmm." He shakes his head sadly. "I think she passed away a few years ago."

"Were she and Mom still friends?"

I see that same look pass across my dad's face again, only this time it's a little more brief. "When she died?" he asks.

"Yeah. That must have been really hard on Mom."

My dad clears his throat. "Yes, well, Julie died after your mother had already, ah, left, so I'm not sure if they were still friends or not."

"But there's a chance they weren't?"

My dad doesn't say anything for a second, just picks up a pen and copies a phone number he's found onto a piece of paper.

"The reason I'm so curious," I forge on, "is because Julie's Brandon's mom," I say.

My dad glances up sharply. He opens his mouth, and for a second I think he's going to pretend to be surprised. But then he just shakes his head and sighs. "Yes," he says, "I know."

"You *knew*?" I take the last bite of my granola bar. "Why didn't you tell me?"

"I don't know." My dad takes a deep breath. "I suppose I didn't think it was that important." What he means is, not important enough to talk about, because in order to do that, he'd have to bring up my mom. I stay quiet, waiting for him to say something else. And after a moment he does. "You two were born right around the same time."

"Us two who?" I ask.

"You and Brandon. Your mom and Julie were still good friends during the time when your mom was pregnant with you. They met in high school and did everything together. In fact, they tried to plan getting pregnant around the same time so that their kids could grow up together."

"And then what happened?" A feeling of dread is rising in my stomach. First of all, I don't like thinking that there could be something to Mrs. Dunham's crazy threats.

It was much more fun when I could just pretend she was an insane ghost. And second, I don't like thinking about anything that has to do with my mom. My mom left. I don't want to spend time getting all upset about it, or wishing I had a mom, or wondering why she did it.

She left. That was *her* choice, and it had nothing to do with me. It's worked well for me to not think about it. And it makes me angry when any information about her comes up in my life. It's like she doesn't have the right. She left, so I don't want her to be able to influence or affect me in any way. Some people would call this denial. I call it being smart.

"Hmm?" my dad asks. He's busy looking down at his paper full of phone numbers.

"What happened? Why weren't they friends anymore?"

He takes a deep breath. "I'm not exactly sure, honey. All this happened right around the time you were born, right before your mom moved out. All I know is that the two of them got into some kind of fight, and they decided not to be friends anymore."

"Who decided?" I ask. "Mom or Julie?"

He shrugs. "I think it was mutual."

I sigh. This is one of those times when having just a dad can be totally frustrating. Doesn't he realize that a breakup, even of just a friendship, is never mutual? Something happened between those two, and it was probably something horrible. It had to be. Otherwise, why would Mrs. Dunham want me to stay away from her son?

I get up and toss my granola bar wrapper into the trash, then turn around to ask my dad another question, but he's on the phone with an electrician. Great. Not only does it seem like this discussion is closed, but now I have the super-fun task of doing my hair without any electricity. This day just keeps getting better and better.

Lyra accosts me during lunch. "So did you find anything else out?" she demands.

I just stare at her. First of all, she just told me something last night and she expects me to already have a plan? God, the youth of today think they are so entitled. Not to mention that she's asked me a question in front of everyone at my lunch table, when she knows full well I'm not going to be able to answer it.

There really should be someone who explains the rules of ghost etiquette to the ghosts before they get sent to me. Like some kind of ghost mediator or something. And then I could grade the ghosts and mark them off if they were being compliant or not. Kind of like a progress report, or an evaluation.

I'd use a red pen (or maybe purple), and all the ghosts would be scared of me and would be all, *What are you writing about me, Kendall?* and *Please don't put down bad things about me, Kendall.* Then I would actually have some power over them.

"I'm going to get a juice," Brandon declares, standing up from the table. "Anyone else want anything?"

"No, thanks," I say.

Kyle and Ellie shake their heads. We're sitting at our normal table in the middle of the cafeteria. It's the perfect table for us, because it's one of those round ones with only four chairs. We snagged it last week and made it our own. And it's cool because we can talk about whatever we want without having to worry about other people listening.

Not that Kyle's talking to me right now. He's still mad, I guess, even though Brandon explained to him what happened and told him that we're now officially a couple.

"You want some Oreos, Kyle?" I ask. I packed a bunch of extra ones this morning because I know they're his favorite. Everything in the fridge was off-limits, but I did manage to find an unopened jar of peanut butter in the pantry. So I have a peanut butter sandwich, chips, an orange, and tons of Oreos.

"No, thank you," he says. But I can see him eyeing the cookies.

"You sure?" I say. "They're Double Stuf. You can lick out the frosting if you want and throw the cookie part away. I don't mind."

"That's wasting," Ellie reports. But I shoot her a look to

let her know that it's not about wasting, that Kyle can waste whatever he wants as long as he forgives me. I can't have Brandon's best friend being mad at me. It's not good.

"Well, okay," Kyle says, reaching across the table. I meant for him to share the cookies with me, but instead he grabs the whole baggie and gets to work eating out the icing.

Whatever. It's probably not good for me to have too much sugar, anyway. I'm already on edge as it is, not to mention the two coffees I had this morning in the English office.

"Are those Double Stuf Oreos?" a sickly sweet voice behind me says. I turn around to see Madison Baker standing there.

She's wearing a short poofy hot pink skirt and a soft-looking white sweater that's so tight, she must have bought it in a size smaller than she needs. A pink headband pulls her hair back from her face, and her makeup is perfect—soft and smoky eye shadow, a slick of seashell-pink gloss, and a swipe of blush. Her skin is flawless—no pimples, no red marks, not even a freckle. I'm torn between really hating her and wanting to ask her what kind of makeup she uses.

I decide on hating her. Not because she's so pretty (but, let's face it, that doesn't help), but because she told my boyfriend I was flirting with another guy.

"Yeah," Kyle says. He holds a cookie out to her. "You want one?"

Ugh. Why would he offer her a cookie? I just want her to go away. And judging from the look on Ellie's face, she wants her to go away too.

"Where does that girl get her makeup?" Lyra asks, peering at Madison. God, I almost forgot Lyra was there. It's actually a little depressing, thinking about a girl who likes your boyfriend having such perfect makeup that even ghosts want to know how she does it.

"No, I don't want any Oreos," Madison says. "They're filled with tons of bad things, like high-fructose corn syrup and trans fat. Anyone who eats those things is just ingesting poison."

Kyle shrugs, and I see Ellie visibly relax. No way Kyle is going to be interested in a girl who talks down about things like trans fats and high-fructose corn syrup, no matter how amazing her cosmetics are.

Then Madison sits down in the seat next to me. The seat where Brandon was just sitting. What? Why? If she doesn't want any Oreos, then why is she sitting down? Actually, why is she here at all?

"Someone's sitting there," I say helpfully.

"Oh, I know," she says. She drums her perfectly painted nails on the table. Obviously, she redid her manicure after the trip to Lyra's mom's salon. No way they did that good a job. "I was just coming over to ask Brandon about the math homework."

"Brandon's not here," I say, reaching into my bag and pulling out my assignment book. "But I can give you the assignment."

"Oh, I know the assignment," she says. She pulls her headband off and shakes her hair out. Soft blond waves cascade down around her shoulders. She looks like a Disney princess. Or a Barbie doll. One of those really annoying fashion ones, not the cool doctor Barbies or anything like that. "I had a question about one of the problems."

"I can help you," I say. The faster I can get her out of here the better. The last thing I want is Brandon coming back to the table and finding Madison here. Although if he does, she'll have to leave, since there will be no place for her to sit.

"I kind of want someone who's good at math," she says. "No offense." She gives me a sweet smile. Ugh. Everyone knows that whenever you say "no offense" to someone, it really means that you're saying something mean and you just want to make it seem like you're not being mean when you totally are.

Madison reaches into her bag and pulls out a Diet Coke. She pops open the top and takes a dainty sip.

"You're not supposed to have soda at school," Kyle says. "Just so you know."

Madison rolls her eyes, like she can't believe how ridiculous that rule is. Then she takes another sip of her soda, not even trying to hide it.

Ellie and I lock eyes over the table, and she shrugs. We all just sit there for a minute or so, not saying anything. It's actually getting awkward, if you want to know the truth.

"Wow," Madison says, "I didn't know I was sitting at the party table. You guys are just so talkative. How do you ever get any eating done?"

Then she picks up Brandon's yogurt, pulls the spoon out of his lunch bag, and starts eating it!

"That's Brandon's yogurt," Kyle says, and I shoot him a grateful smile.

"I'm sure he won't mind," Madison says wickedly. She licks the spoon, and I'm pretty sure it's not my imagination that she glances at me out of the corner of her eye with a smarmy look.

"Wow," Lyra says. She sits down on the table pretty much on top of Brandon's lunch. "That girl is eating your boyfriend's yogurt. Talk about being aggressive." She gets really close to her and peers at her face. "How *does* she get her skin to look like that?"

Brandon returns to the table before I can figure out what to do.

"Hey," he says, "what's going on?" I wait for him to say something about Madison eating his yogurt, but she's put the carton back down on the table, like she hasn't just been stealing someone else's lunch. I meet Brandon's eye and throw a pointed glance at his yogurt, hoping he'll look at it and be all, *Who was eating my yogurt without permission?* But he doesn't get the hint.

"I just needed some help with my math," Madison says.

"Oh," Brandon says. "Well, you can always stay after and get someone in the math lab to help you. They're there pretty much every day after the bell rings."

"There's just this one problem on the homework that's been giving me trouble," Madison says, ignoring his comment about the math lab. "And I really need to get a good grade. Otherwise Mr. Jacobi is going to kill me."

I reach into my baggie to take out a chip, and then find that I've crumbled it in my hand. I wait for Brandon to tell her he can't help her.

Instead he says, "Do you have your textbook?"

"It's in my locker," she says, and smiles up at him. "Will you come with me to get it? Then we can go over the problem."

"I don't know," Brandon says doubtfully. "I'm eating lunch with Kendall." He puts his hand on my shoulder. Yay! Score one for me and Brandon!

"Oh, I'm sure Kendall doesn't mind," Madison says, looking at me and giving me another sickly sweet smile. "Do you, Kendall?"

Great. Now if I say I do mind, I'm the jealous, insecure girlfriend. And if I say I don't, Brandon is going to waltz out of here with Madison. "I don't mind," I say, hoping my voice doesn't sound too strangled.

"Are you sure?" Brandon asks. "Because I don't have to." He's looking at me with concern, and I know he's thinking about how upset I was about Madison calling him. Well, this is my chance to prove that I'm a confident and secure girlfriend.

"I'm sure," I say. Not.

Brandon balls up his lunch bag and then dumps all his garbage into the trash can against the wall. He comes back to the table and gives me a quick kiss. "I'll be right back, okay? Maybe the three of us can go over the problem together."

"Sure." I shrug like it's no big deal, even though my heart is beating fast in my chest and I have a lump in my throat. Why is he leaving with her? Why couldn't she go get the book by herself? And besides, doesn't he realize that she made up a big lie about me and Micah? Why is he still talking to her?

I watch as Brandon and Madison approach the lunch monitor and Madison starts explaining the situation. We're not allowed to leave the caf during lunch unless we have permission. A second later the lunch monitor nods, and Madison and Brandon slip out into the hallway.

"You okay?" Ellie asks once Brandon's gone.

"I'm fine," I say, giving her a smile. "They'll be right back anyway."

But they're not right back. In fact, by the time the bell rings, signaling the end of the period, Brandon and Madison haven't returned.

I don't see Brandon for the rest of the day, and by the time the bus drops me off in front of my house, I'm really annoyed. I mean, yes, he did send me a text saying that Madison had left her book in Mr. Jacobi's room, and by the time they went up to get it, the lunch period was over. But still.

Did he really have to go with Madison to Mr. Jacobi's room? Yeah, it was only for ten minutes or so. And it's not like I needed him for anything. It wasn't like he left me stranded at the mall or stood me up for a date or something. But still. It's polite and cordial behavior to come back if you told someone that you're coming back.

I think Lyra knows I'm upset, because even though she rides the bus home with me, she doesn't say a word the whole time. When I get off the bus, I head right for the cemetery. I take a walk around, and then sit on the bench near my grandmother's grave for a while. Being close to her always makes me feel a lot better, although today it's not making me feel as good as I thought it would.

When I get back to my house, Cindy's there with my dad. They're both at the kitchen table, eating soup.

"Hi, Kendall," Cindy says warmly.

"Hi." Great. Talk about the last person I want to see. I know I said I wasn't mad at her anymore, and I'm not. I mean, it's not her fault she's in love with my dad and he decided not to tell me. I'm not her daughter. But I'm already not in the best mood.

So how am I supposed to be nice to her?

"Would you like some soup?" my dad asks.

"No, thanks." I hate tomato soup. There's nothing in it. No noodles, no vegetables, not even rice. Why not just eat sauce?

"Are you sure?" Cindy asked. "I made it myself."

She's looking at me with a super-hopeful look, like she wants me to eat her stupid soup so bad that she can't take it.

"Fine," I say, sighing. "I'll have some soup."

I grab a loaf of Italian bread out of the bread box and cut myself a thick slice. Then I slather it with butter. Hopefully, I can use it to sop up most of the soup. I sit down at the table, and my dad sets a steaming bowl in front of me. "Thanks," I say. And then I realize that the power is on.

"Hey," I say, "they fixed the lights!"

"Yup," my dad says happily. "Apparently there was some kind of surge or something that caused the whole box to fry."

Yikes. The whole box to fry? That sounds serious.

"It was going to cost me two thousand dollars to get it fixed."

I almost spit tomato soup all over the table. "Two thousand dollars? Do we even have two thousand dollars?"

"Well, luckily we didn't have to worry about that, because Cindy saved the day." My dad smiles at her across the table.

"I have a friend whose husband is an electrician," she says, waving her hand in the air like it's no big deal. "And so he gave your father a deal."

"He said he'd never seen anything like it," my dad says. He gets up to cut himself a slice of bread. "He said it was the weirdest thing, and he doesn't have any idea how anything like that could have happened."

"Wow," I say. "Um, maybe we have bad wiring in this house." Or, you know, a crazy ghost who might be dangerous and here to get some sort of revenge on her ex–best friend. I take another bite of my bread.

I wonder if Mrs. Dunham's so determined to keep me away from Brandon that she'd do anything, even hurt me. I always thought ghosts couldn't do that, because they can't touch people. But obviously she has some kind of power to surge electricity through people's houses. Who knows what else she can do? And who knows what she was *trying* to do? Maybe she wanted to start a fire. Oh my God. Does Mrs. Dunham want to kill me?

What the hell did my mom do to her, anyway? And why won't my dad give me any more information about it? I watch him out of the corner of my eye as he ladles more soup into his bowl. Hmm.

He's obviously very good at keeping secrets. I mean, think about how long he kept the whole thing with Cindy a secret. He's sneaky, that one. I should have known it when I caught him putting a slice of cheese onto his egg-white omelette a few months ago even though his doctor specifi-cally told him that he needs to limit his saturated fat intake because of his high cholesterol.

I'm so caught up in thinking about what crazy things Mrs. Dunham could do that at first I don't realize that Cindy is talking to me.

". . . do you know what I mean?"

I swallow my spoonful of tomato soup and wonder if it would be rude to ask her to repeat whatever it is she said. "I'm sorry," I say. "I was just so into eating this delicious soup that I got distracted. What did you say?"

"I said that I know your dad has talked to you about our relationship, and that you said you're okay with it." She sets her spoon down and then twists her hands in her lap nervously. "I want you to know that I really appreciate your reaction. I'm sure this can't be easy for you."

"Thanks, Cindy," I say.

She visibly relaxes, and I feel kind of bad for how hard

I've been on her. She was obviously nervous about talking to me just then. She probably thought I was going to yell and scream at her. The truth is, she's always been nice to me, and she's trying to be nice to me right now. It can't be that fun to be in love with a guy who has a teenage daughter.

I wonder if they'll get married. Ooh, I'll probably get to be in the wedding! I mean, how can they really leave me out? I'm the daughter of the groom. I'll definitely get to be a bridesmaid. And I'll probably get to have my hair and makeup professionally done. Probably by one of those makeup-and-hair people that come right to your house.

And I'll get to wear a really flowing gown, with lots of sequins or fake flowers or something. I wonder if I can talk Cindy into having her wedding color be purple. That would be so pretty, a purple wedding. And I could wear an orchid in my hair, and then—

"Hello!" Lyra yells, appearing in front of me. "Are you going to help me or not?"

I sigh and take the last spoonful of my tomato soup. "Dad," I say, "do you mind if I walk into town for a little while?"

Chapter

9

"Wow!" Sharon says when she sees me walking into the salon. "Our best customer is back!"

"Well, probably second best," Micah says, looking up from where he's reading a sports magazine at one of the nail stations.

His mother shoots him a look. I try not to feel offended. Who's their first best customer? There can't really be anyone who comes in here more than me, can there? I mean, no offense to Sharon, because she's really nice, but let's face it—this salon is kind of awful. And when I say "kind of," I mean, you know, "totally."

"Yup," I say, wandering over to the nail polish shelf and looking at the bottles. "It's me. I'm back."

"Well, we have a new shade that you might be interested in," Sharon says.

Oh, thank God. It would definitely be weird to ask them to put on the exact same color as last time.

"Also, you should know that we've had to raise our prices, to, ah, accommodate for some unexpected administrative costs," Sharon says. "So manicures are now two dollars more than they were previously."

"Yeah, if you count lack of customers as administrative costs," Micah chimes in.

"Micah!" Sharon scolds.

"It's okay," I say. "I understand all about, ah, administrative costs. My dad has his own construction business."

"Wonderful!" Sharon says. "Now let me show you our new color." She pulls it out of some box she has hiding behind the register, like she's presenting something really huge. She sets the bottle of nail polish down on the counter with a flourish. "Isn't it something?"

I peer at it. "Oh, yeah," I say. "It's something, all right." If by "something" you mean a puke-green color I wouldn't be caught dead in.

"Would you like to try it?" She cocks her head. "I'll give you a dollar off if you promise to tell all your friends where you got it."

Oh, God. I stare at her. She can't really think it's a good color, can she? And that my friends would just be clamoring to come in here and get it? Is she really that clueless?

Lyra shakes her head next to me. "Yes," she says, "my mom is really that clueless. But her heart's in the right place."

"It's gorgeous," I lie. "But I think I'm going to stick with something a little more, ah, red. That way it will match my outfit for tomorrow."

"Are you sure?" Sharon's face falls. "Maybe you could wear something different."

"I told you no one was going to like that color, Mom," Micah says. He shakes his head without looking up from his magazine. I catch a glimpse of a BMX bike on one of the pages.

"I don't understand," Sharon says. "The salesman said this was a very hot color for fall." She stares at the bottle, perplexed.

"Poor Mom," Lyra says, her voice catching. "First she has to lose me, and now this."

Oh, for the love of . . . "On second thought I will take that color," I say, picking up the bottle. "It's a nice shade of, um, green, and I'm sure I can find an outfit that will match it." Not.

"Really?" Sharon's eyes widen. "Wonderful!" She turns around and gives Micah a satisfied look.

"Now," she says, "I have an appointment booked for

four thirty, but Micah would be happy to get started on your nails, wouldn't you, Micah?"

Micah doesn't answer. He's totally absorbed in whatever article he's reading. "Micah!" his mom yells.

"Oh, yeah, yes, definitely," he says, rolling his eyes and putting his magazine away.

I sit down in the chair. And then I think about what Brandon said to me earlier. About how I was flirting with Micah. Which I so wasn't. But still.

"Maybe we can skip the hand massage today," I say. "I'm, um, kind of in a hurry."

"Sure," he says, taking the bottle of lotion and setting it under the counter. I watch longingly as it disappears. Good-bye, pear-and-vanilla-scented goodness. I'll miss you.

"So," he whispers once he's done taking off my nail polish. "Did you really like this green color, or did you just pick it to be nice to my mom?"

"I really like it," I say quickly.

But he just grins at me, like he knows I'm lying.

"Ask him about Rachel," Lyra commands. "Ask him why she's up all night crying and clutching her phone."

I roll my eyes. Yeah, great idea. I'll just bust out with, *Oh, hey, Micah, I know I'm a perfect stranger and all, but what's going on with your dead sister's friend Rachel? Why is she crying all night in her room? What? How do I know all this? Oh, don't worry about it. Just give me the info.*

"I'm sorry if I'm a little slow at this," Micah says. "I'm going to get better. At least, if my mom has anything to do with it." He sighs and dips the brush into the polish. And then I realize he thought I was rolling my eyes at him for being slow.

"Oh, no," I say. "I wasn't rolling my eyes at you. I was rolling my eyes at . . ." Something tells me "the ghost of your dead sister" isn't going to go over too well. "This memory of this girl at my school."

"Really?" he asks. "What did she do?"

"Ah, well, she . . ." I rack my brains trying to remember something cringe-worthy that happened at school. I roll my eyes probably a million times during the course of a school day, and yet now, when I need to remember an example of one of those times, my mind goes blank. The same thing happens to me when I'm taking a math test. It's like I know how to do the problems, and then, when the test starts, whoosh, all the info goes right out of my head.

"She what?" Micah prompts.

"She, well, you know, she um . . . she dropped her hot lunch all over the floor."

"Oh." Micah frowns. And doesn't really laugh or anything. Not that I can blame him. Rolling your eyes because someone dropped their lunch is a pretty bratty thing to do.

We lapse into an awkward silence. I look around to see

141

if there are any family pictures or if there's any way I can bring Lyra into the conversation.

"Ask him about me," she says again. She tries to poke me, but of course it's no use. "Go on," she says. "Ask him."

"So," I say, "do you have any funny school stories to tell me?"

"School stories?" Lyra asks. "Why are you asking him about school stories? Ask him about me!"

"Um, or maybe some family stories," I try. "Like something funny that happened in your family?"

"I don't have any school stories," he says. He takes a cotton ball and soaks it in nail polish remover, then gets to work removing the nail polish from my other hand. Which isn't exactly the way you're supposed to do it. Normally you're supposed to remove the nail polish from both hands first, and then get to work filing and polishing. He's trying to do it one nail at a time, I think. Hmm. It's definitely illegal for him to work here. Like, for real.

"Why not?" I say. "What was your old school like? In your old town?"

"How did you know I have an old town?" he asks.

"Huh?"

"How did you know I just moved here?"

"Oh, good job," Lyra says. "Now he's going to think you're some kind of nutter."

Oh, *now* she's worried about me seeming crazy. She

didn't seem worried about it a little while ago, when she was trying to get me to just bring up things that I should technically have no idea about.

"Well, I just assumed you had," I say, "since you would probably go to my school and I, um, haven't seen you around."

"Well, that's going to change," Micah says. "I'm starting there tomorrow."

"Cool." Hmm. Is it my imagination or is he starting with the hand rub again? "You don't have to do the whole hand massage thing," I remind him. "I'm kind of on a time schedule."

"Oh, great," Lyra says. "Tell him you're on a time schedule, real smart. Then what's going to happen if you actually do start talking to him? Then what? You're going to have to get out of here?"

"It's okay," Micah says, still looking at me. "I don't mind giving you a quick hand massage. It won't take long."

Wow. He's actually kind of looking at me . . . I don't know, *weird*. Like . . . the way Kyle was looking at Ellie the first time we all hung out and he was trying to flirt with her. But that's ridiculous. Micah can't be flirting with me. A, because he hardly knows me. And B, because boys don't usually flirt with me.

Seriously, before I met Brandon, my experience with boys was, like, none. And when I say "like, none" I really mean "completely none." So I can't imagine why all of a sudden Micah would start flirting with me. Unless it's one of those things where you get a boyfriend and then tons of boys start finding you attractive. I've heard about things like that happening. It's like some weird rule of the universe or something. Just the other day Ellie was telling me about how this friend of her mom's has this super-hot son who tried to hold her hand at some family get-together. It was a total scandal.

"So, do you have any brothers and sisters?" I blurt, and pull my hand back like it's on fire.

Micah looks startled, but he recovers smoothly. "I have a sister," he says. "Actually, I had a sister. She died." He just blurts it out like it's nothing. But then his eyes start to look a little watery.

"That's awful," I say. "How did she die?"

"She had a heart defect," he says. "She had it since she was born."

"I knew it was my heart!" Lyra says.

"That's so sad," I say, pretending to be horrified. "Were you guys close?"

"Yeah," he says. "I mean, she drove me crazy, but we were friends." He's trying to put on a brave face, the way that guys do, but I can tell he's really upset about it. It's really sad. And sweet.

"That's nice," I say. "I'll bet she was a good sister."

"Oh, Lyra was good at everything she did," he says. He

points over at a picture of her that's hanging on the wall. "That was last year, when she won the school science fair. She was competing against eighth and ninth graders, and she still won."

"Wow," I say.

"Like it was hard," Lyra says, walking over and peering at the picture. "Those high schoolers don't know anything about science." She leans down and looks at the photograph even closer. "I look really good in that picture," she says. "It was because I'd just had my hair done."

"Yeah, she was a great sister, a great daughter, a great friend."

I sit up, sensing an opening. "Oh, really?" I say. "Did she have a lot of friends?"

"She didn't have a ton of friends," Micah says. "But the friends she did have were really close to her." He's removing the polish on my left pinkie nail. I try not to think about the fact that he's still touching my hand, even though he's not technically giving me a massage.

"Oh, that's cool," I say. "I'll bet she was a really good best friend."

"Yeah." Micah nods. "Her best friend was this girl named Rachel. They were always pulling pranks on me and my friend Nick." He grins, remembering.

"We were not!" Lyra yells. "You guys were always pulling pranks on us."

"That's cool," I say. "Does Rachel live in your old hometown?"

Micah nods, then very carefully paints my pinkie finger with that disgusting green color. "Yeah. But her family is still really close with mine. They're actually coming over for dinner this weekend."

Lyra gasps out loud.

I gasp out loud.

"Oh," Micah says. "I'm sorry. Did I hurt you?" He drops my hand. "Sometimes I get a little too rough."

"Oh, no," I say. "I was just, ah, thinking that it must be really nice to be able to have your sister's friend over. You know, like it might remind you of her."

"I guess." He frowns and keeps painting. He's also giving me a weird look. I guess the whole remembering-his-sister part of the afternoon is over. Not to mention the fact that he's not flirting with me anymore. Like, at all.

"You have to get yourself invited to that dinner!" Lyra yells. "It's important. Immediately! Go on, ask him!"

Oh my God. I thought she was supposed to be smart. I'm really going to have to explain to her later about how not to stalk boys. Not to mention that she must realize that I can't talk to her while other people are around. And yet for some ridiculous reason she keeps talking to me.

"Oh, that sounds fun," I say. "Um—"

The bells on the salon door tinkle.

"That must be my four thirty appointment!" I hear Sharon exclaim from her spot behind the cash register. "Right on time. There's my favorite customer!"

I turn around to see who this alleged first, best customer is. Especially since she's now apparently Sharon's favorite as well. Whoever it is must be crazy. Probably some kind of senile old woman who doesn't know that yellowish green is not a good color for nails.

"Hi, Sharon!" a girl's voice squeals.

Huh. So I guess it's not a crazy old woman after all.

"I'm ready for my manicure!"

That voice sounds familiar, but I can't quite place it.

It hits me a second before I see her.

Madison Baker, waltzing into the back of the salon and sitting right down at the other nail station.

"Hello, Kendall," she says when she sees me. She gives me a knowing smile. The kind of smile you give someone when you've been trying to catch them doing something and now you've caught them doing something.

"Oh, hi, Madison," I say, trying to keep my voice from catching.

"I see you're having a nice time," she says, looking at me and Micah.

"Um, not really," I say nonchalantly. "I'm just, you know, getting my nails done."

"Me too. But I always have Sharon do mine." God, she's

so transparent. She always has Sharon do hers? The place just opened. How many times could she possibly have had Sharon do her nails? And besides, it's so obvious that the only reason Madison's here is to hopefully catch me with Micah. Which she's done, but still.

"Yeah, well, I wanted Sharon to do mine, too, but she said she had an appointment."

"Yeah, I'll bet you did," Madison says. She cracks her gum and then pulls her phone out of her purse and takes her time sending a text. "Does Brandon know you're here?" she asks. The side of her mouth slides up into a sly grin.

"Of course he does," I say.

"Oh, really?" she asks. "That's good. So if I happen to mention it to him, he won't be surprised."

And then she turns her back to me, signaling that the conversation is over.

The rest of my day is a big mess.

Here are the reasons:

1. Lyra keeps yelling at me about how I messed everything up by not getting myself invited over to her house when Rachel is going to be there. Even when I point out that I hardly even know her brother, she doesn't want to listen. She just keeps going on and on about how it's

my last chance to see Rachel and figure out what's going on. Which is ridiculous. Lyra's only been here a few days. When I explain that to her calmly, and then ask her to please stop talking to me in front of people, because, hello, I can't answer her, she gets all annoyed and acts like I'm being completely unreasonable. Then she disappears.

2. Ellie gets grounded for the night, and her mom takes away her cell phone. I'm not sure exactly why, but from what I could gather, it had something to do with Ellie staying up too late, talking on the phone with Kyle when she was supposed to be sleeping. So I had no one to obsess with about what happened today in the salon.

3. Brandon doesn't call me all night, and when he finally does, I try to tell him about how I went to get my nails done again today. I want to make sure that he doesn't hear it from Madison before I have a chance to tell him. But when I tell him, he gets all annoyed with me.

He keeps asking me why I have to get my nails done there, and I tell him that it's close to my house and it's cheap. So then Brandon says that maybe we should just talk about this the next day at school, and so then I say okay. By the time I hang up the phone, I'm feeling sad and confused.

Needless to say, I get a horrible night's sleep. I toss and turn the whole night, lying in my bed, waiting to see if Mrs. Dunham is going to show up. She doesn't, which is a relief.

But still. When I wake up, I feel totally out of sorts. I don't even feel like doing my hair, which is so not like me. I put it in two French braids. Then I tie two ribbons at the bottom of each braid. Red and black. I hope the neat style is going to make me feel like my life is orderly.

When I get downstairs, I pour myself some cereal. My dad went out last night and did some grocery shopping, replacing all the food that spoiled while the power was out.

"What's wrong?" he asks when he sees me.

"Nothing," I say. "Just tired, I guess."

"Okay." He looks a little nervous, like maybe he's afraid I'm going to do something crazy, like, you know, freak out about him and Cindy again. But if he's worried about that, he really shouldn't be. I have way bigger problems. Problems I obviously can't talk to him about.

When I get to school, Ellie's waiting for me outside the front entrance.

"Oh my God," she says. "I'm so sorry about last night. My mom was being completely unreasonable."

"She took your phone away?"

Ellie nods. "She said I was up too late talking to Kyle. Which is ridiculous. Midnight is not too late. And besides, it's not like he keeps me awake. If I wasn't talking to him, I'd be doing something else. She treats me like I'm a baby, and it's so not fair."

"Yeah," I say. I know it probably sounds mean, but I'm not really in the mood for Ellie's story about how her mom took her phone away. I mean, no offense, but Ellie not being able to talk to Kyle until midnight is not exactly a reason to get all upset.

"So, what's up?" Ellie reaches into her bag and pulls out a bottle of water, then takes a long sip. "Is something going on?"

"Sort of," I say. "I just . . ." I take a deep breath, and then I realize I have no idea how I'm going to explain this to her. What am I going to say? That Brandon's mad at me because Madison Baker saw me at the salon with Micah? Ellie's going to want to know why I keep going to that ridiculous salon.

She's already suspicious, and honestly, I don't blame her. I'd be suspicious too if she kept wanting to go back there when they obviously don't know what they're doing.

I can't tell her about the ghosts. I can't tell her about

Mrs. Dunham. I can't tell anyone about anything, and it's really upsetting.

"Kendall, what's wrong?" Ellie asks. And she looks so concerned about me that I can't take it anymore. And before I know what's happening, I burst into tears.

"Come on," Ellie says, grabbing my arm and leading me toward the school. "You need sugar."

We skip first period. I know it's bad. I've actually never skipped a class before, except for one time when I got my schedule mixed up and ended up in gym instead of science. (Don't ask.)

But if I get in trouble, I don't care. I don't see how things could get worse than they are right now.

Ellie takes me to a little alcove under the stairs by the math lab, and then spreads out a blanket on the floor.

"Where'd you get a blanket?" I ask.

"Oh, I always keep a blanket in my locker," she says. "The rooms in this school are always so cold."

"Oh."

"So," she says. She reaches into her bag and pulls out a doughnut.

"Where'd you get a doughnut?" I ask.

"I got three of them," she says. "I bought them from the cafeteria."

I frown. "The cafeteria is open?"

"It is if you know who to talk to."

Wow. Who knew that Ellie was so resourceful? The doughnut is one of those prepackaged ones that has white powdered sugar that gets all over the place, but beggars can't be choosers.

"Wow, Ellie," I say, "you're kind of turning into a rebel."

She smiles. "Now," she says. "Tell me what the heck is going on."

I open my doughnut and take a small bite. "Well," I say, deciding how much I should reveal. "Brandon and I are having problems."

"What kind of problems?"

"I think he might like Madison Baker."

"No way." Ellie shakes her head. "He definitely doesn't like Madison Baker."

"How do you know?" I ask, my heart soaring just a little. "Did Kyle say something?"

"Well, no," she admits. "But how could he like Madison Baker? She's so . . . so . . . *horrible*."

"I know," I say. "But guys always like horrible girls. It's, like, a rule or something. I mean, it's the basis of pretty much every romantic movie in existence. Only, in movies the guy always ends up with the right girl."

"Brandon likes you," she says. "You guys are perfect for each other."

"Maybe," I say.

"Look, you just have to stop making it so complicated," she says. "You can't always have everything perfect, and when things come up, you have to talk to Brandon about them."

"Yeah," I say, even though that's obviously not going to happen. Can you imagine? *Oh, hi, Brandon. I'm sorry but I had to go to that salon because I'm helping a ghost whose brother works there. Oh, and by the way, the ghost of your mother is stalking me and it might have something to do with my mother, and she totally made all the lights in my house go out.*

The sound of footsteps on the staircase above us comes echoing down the hall, and Ellie and I hold our breath and stay quiet. After a few minutes the sound starts getting fainter, and I breathe a sigh of relief.

"You need to just work on being honest with him," Ellie says. "Like I am with Kyle."

My eyes fill up with tears again. The thing is, I wish I could be honest with Brandon. I wish I could be honest with everyone. But I can't. And I think that's the thing that's hurting me the most. It's kind of like my whole life is a complete lie.

"Oh, Kendall," Ellie says, and she hugs me.

"I'm okay," I say, forcing a smile. "I'm just being dramatic. You know how I can get."

"Yeah," she says. But she's looking at me with concern, and I can tell that she doesn't fully believe me.

Ellie opens her mouth to say something, but before she can, the bell rings.

"We should go to second period," I say, gathering up the doughnut wrappers. I can already hear the sound of footsteps thundering down the stairs as our classmates get out of class.

"Okay," Ellie says. She stands up and starts to fold up the blanket. "It's going to be okay, Kendall," she says. "I promise."

"Thanks, Ellie. I know it is." I paste a smile on my face and hope she believes me.

When we walk out into the hall, a crazy thing happens.

I see Micah wandering around by the science rooms. He's holding his schedule and peering down at it, confused. Almost like he doesn't know exactly where he's going. Which would make sense, since he's new to our school.

It takes me a second to realize it's him, like when you see someone out of their normal environment. It's like he shouldn't be here, at school with me. He should be back at the salon, sitting behind the nail counter.

"Hey," Ellie says. "Isn't that the guy from the salon?"

"Hey!" Micah says, raising his hand when he sees us. "What are you guys up to?"

"Just, you know, at school," Ellie says.

"Hi, Kendall," Micah says. He looks down at my hands

and then picks one of them up and looks at it. He has very soft hands, for a boy. Not that I've touched that many boys' hands. But still. "What happened to your green nail polish?" he asks.

"Oh," I say. "Um, I accidentally chipped a nail, so I had to, um, take it off."

"What green nail polish?" Ellie asks. "You didn't tell me you were getting green polish. When did you buy it?"

"Oh, she didn't buy it," Micah reports. He's still holding up my hand and looking at my nails. It's actually kind of uncomfortable, if you want to know the truth. But I can't just take my hand back. That would be rude. Wouldn't it? Since when is he so into hands, anyway? I mean, usually at the salon he acts like he kind of doesn't know what he's doing. Now suddenly he's all into hands?

"What do you mean, she didn't buy it?" Ellie asks. She's looking at me suspiciously.

"I mean that she came into the salon." Micah has a twinkle in his eye now.

"You went to the salon again?" Ellie asks. Her eyes are practically bugging out of her head.

"Kendall comes in a lot," Micah says. He's not looking at my hand anymore, but he's still holding it. And now he's sort of . . . ah, caressing my fingers.

"Oh, really?" Ellie says, crossing her arms over her chest. "She comes in a lot, does she?"

"Well," Micah says, and gives me a grin. "It's probably not just for the manicures."

And then the most horrible thing I could image happening happens. While I'm standing there in the hallway, with Micah basically holding my hand, Brandon steps out of his science class.

"Hey," he says happily when he sees me. But then he sees Micah. And our hands. His eyes darken, and it looks almost like a storm cloud is moving over his face. "Who's this?" he asks.

I immediately pull my hand away from Micah's. But it's too late. The damage has been done. Brandon has already seen it.

"Oh, this is just my friend," I say, making sure to put emphasis on the word "friend."

Brandon comes over and puts his arm around me. "I'm Brandon," he says. "I'm Kendall's boyfriend."

"Oh." Micah looks startled. Probably he never thought about the fact that I might have a boyfriend. And honestly, why would he? He apparently thought I was coming into the salon because I had a big crush on him. That thought never even occurred to me, but when you think about it, it totally makes sense. No one needs to get their nails done that often. So you'd need some kind of other reason for going in. And what other reason would that be besides a ridiculous crush on the owner's son?

"Oh," a voice calls out from halfway down the hall. "Look at that! It's Micah from the salon!"

I turn around to see Madison Baker waltzing down the hall toward us. Great. Talk about a bunch of bad luck. What are the chances that Brandon would come out of his classroom, and now Madison is here too? It's like some kind of horrible reunion.

"You're Micah from the salon?" Brandon asks. His jaw sets.

"Yeah," Micah says. "I'm Micah. I met Kendall at the nail salon. She comes in a lot." Ohmigod. What the hell is wrong with him? Doesn't he know that when you start to get challenged by a girl's boyfriend, you back off immediately? It's like guy code or something.

"Um," I say quickly, moving closer to Brandon. "I wouldn't call it a *lot*."

"I would," says Madison helpfully. "I mean, every time I go in there, she's there."

I open my mouth to point out that Madison wouldn't know I was there so much if she wasn't there herself, and so maybe she's the one with the big crush on Micah. But before I can, Micah pipes up.

"Yup," he says. "Every time Kendall comes in, I do her nails."

"Yeah, well—," Brandon says, dropping his arm from around my shoulders and taking a step toward Micah.

Luckily, the warning bell rings.

"Oh, well, we need to get to class," I say, taking Brandon's arm and pulling him down the hall.

I shoot a look over my shoulder and give Ellie an *I'll explain this to you later* look, which of course is a halfway lie, because I have no idea how I'm going to explain it to her. As I turn back around, I can see Madison giving me a smug look.

"What the heck was that about?" Brandon asks.

"What do you mean?" I ask, stalling.

"I mean, why was he holding your hand?"

"He wasn't," I say. "I mean, um, he was, but it wasn't like that. He was just checking out my nail polish." I hold my hand up and wiggle my fingers. "See?"

Brandon shakes his head. "Like any guy really cares about what your nail polish looks like. And what were they talking about, you going in there all the time? Is that true?" His voice has stopped being angry, and now he just sounds kind of . . . sad. Like he's really hurt that I would lie to him.

"It's not that often," I say. "I mean, I just like to get my nails done."

"Kendall," he says. "Tell me the truth. Do you like Micah?"

"No." I shake my head. "I swear. I don't like him. I'm not going to go back to the salon again."

The words are out of my mouth before I can stop them. Seriously, it's like I don't know what I'm saying. Obviously I can't promise to never go back to the salon again. How am I going to talk to Micah? Or Sharon? If I can't talk to Lyra's mom and brother, I'm never going to be able to figure out how she can move on.

"I can't ask you to do that," Brandon says. "If you like going to get your nails done, you should get your nails done."

"No," I say, shaking my head. "I'm not going to go back there. Seriously, I promise."

"I told you, you don't have to do that," he says. He takes a deep breath and then runs his fingers through his hair. The final bell rings, signaling that we're supposed to be in class, but neither one of us moves. "Look, I'm sorry I freaked out back there," he says. "I trust you, Kendall. I do."

"Thanks." I take a deep breath. "And I trust you. And I hope you don't believe the things that Madison is telling you. That girl is trouble, Brandon."

"Yeah," he says, "I know." He takes a step toward me, and I feel myself start to blush. "We need a date," he says, grinning. "How about Saturday night? Want to do something? Just the two of us?"

"I'd love to," I breathe.

"Good." He kisses me then, right there in the hall.

And when he pulls back and squeezes my hand, I know everything's going to be all right.

· · ·

I'm in such a good mood that I don't even care when I get in trouble for being late to English. A little lunch detention never hurt anyone, ha-ha.

And besides, it gives me time to come up with a plan.

All (well, most) of my problems are happening because of Micah. And the reason I keep having to hang out with Micah is because of Lyra. But if I can figure out how to get Lyra to move on, then poof! I won't have to see Micah anymore.

The only problem is how I'm going to do that. Especially since I'm not supposed to be going to the salon anymore. I guess I could try to talk to Micah at school or something, but since he's an eighth grader, we're not going to be in any of the same classes. And if I try to talk to him in the hall, there's a chance that Brandon might see us. Or even worse, that Madison will see us. And who knows what kind of story she'll make up about how it looked? She'll probably tell Brandon we were making out or something. Ugh.

Fortunately, the solution to my problem presents itself that afternoon when I get on the bus. I'm the first one on, because I rushed out of school in an effort to avoid Ellie. Since I had lunch detention, I haven't really seen her all day. Of course, she's been texting me nonstop, things like *Kendall! You can't avoid me forever!*

Once I get on the bus, I pull out my phone and type

back, *Sorry! Phone was dying, so I shut it off for a bit. I'm not avoiding you!*

It's horrible to lie. But what choice do I have? It's so hard with Ellie, too, because she knows me probably better than anyone else, even my dad. The only person who even came close to knowing me as well as Ellie was my grandma. So Ellie obviously knows something's up, and so I can't just—

"Can I sit here?" a deep voice asks.

I look up in surprise, ready to tell whoever it is to find their own seat. We're lucky in that our bus is usually pretty empty, and so no one has to sit together unless they really want to. And who wants to sit with someone they don't know? Not me, that's for sure.

"There are tons of empty—," I start to say, but then I stop. Because the voice belongs to Micah. Micah is on my bus! I had no idea. This is perfect! Now I can just talk to him on the bus! And no one will know! "Oh," I say. "Yes, you can sit here."

He plops down next to me. A little *too* next to me, if you know what I mean. I move closer to the window, but there's only so far I can go.

"I didn't know you took this bus," I say.

"Well, it's my first day," he reminds me. "And this morning my mom drove me to school."

"Oh."

"She wanted to meet with my guidance counselor. She's so overprotective ever since my sister died."

"Yeah, boo," Lyra says, appearing in the seat ahead of us. "You get to go to school and be alive and complain about how mom has to take you to the guidance counselor. Some people would kill to go to school."

I want to tell her that she's forgetting that school isn't all it's cracked up to be, but (a) she wouldn't listen, and (b) Micah would think I was crazy.

"Oh, that sucks," I say. "My dad is super-protective too."

"Really?" Micah says. He reaches into his backpack and pulls out a bag of cheese popcorn. He opens it and offers me some. I take a handful. Since I had lunch detention and then hid out in the library, I didn't really have time to eat a proper lunch. "Because he doesn't seem like the type who would be overprotective."

"Why do you say that?" I ask. "You've never met my dad."

"Yeah, but he lets you have a boyfriend. So he must be at least kind of cool."

"Not really," I say. "You should see how he is with Brandon. He gives him a really hard time." The bus has been filling up with kids, and the driver shuts the door and shifts into gear. As we turn out of the school parking lot, Micah gets jostled and his leg pushes up against mine.

"So how come you didn't tell me you had a boyfriend?" he asks.

"Oh, I don't know," I say nonchalantly. "I guess it just never really came up."

"Right," he says. But he says it like *Riiiiight, you're lying,* not like *Right, that makes sense.* And he has a twinkle in his eye and a little bit of a knowing look on his face.

I must look confused, because Lyra feels the need to explain things to me.

"He thinks you didn't tell him because you like him," she says. "I mean, he thinks you like *him,* Micah. Not Brandon. He thinks every girl likes him." She frowns. "Mostly because they usually do. He's used to getting whatever girl he wants. So he just thinks everyone likes him."

Hmm. Well, she could have mentioned that before she sent me off to get my nails done by him. Here I was, sitting there totally innocent and completely clueless while he was giving me hand massages. And the whole time he was probably thinking that I was coming into the salon just to see him. Which I was, but not for the reason he thinks.

I open my mouth to tell him I don't like him like that, and that I'm sorry if he's gotten the wrong idea. I don't even feel bad about it. Someone as good-looking as Micah is going to have no problem finding other girls. Maybe I can hook him up with Madison Baker, get her out of my hair.

"Micah—"

"No!" Lyra screams. "You can't tell him you don't like him! If you do, he's going to completely lose interest in you."

I frown. "And why would that be a bad thing?" I say out loud.

"What?" Micah asks, confused.

"Uh, nothing," I say quickly. "Just, um, talking to myself."

He frowns.

"It will be a bad thing because then he won't want to hang out with you!" Lyra yells. "He doesn't want to hang out with any girls that aren't interested in him. He's like a walking hormone."

"So," Micah says. "What are you up to this weekend?"

"Hanging out with my boyfriend," I say quickly. I don't want to lead the poor boy on. "What are you up to?"

He shrugs. "Tomorrow I have this stupid family dinner thing," he says. "I think I told you about it. My mom's best friend is coming over with her daughter, Rachel. But after that I'm totally free."

"Tell him to invite you!" Lyra yells. She's jumping all around in the seat ahead of me. She's moving so fast that I'm afraid she's going to actually move the seat, even though I know that's impossible. "Pretend you like him!" she screams again. Her glasses almost fly off her nose, she's bouncing so hard. Jeez. I've never seen someone so excited before.

I sigh.

"So, ah," I say, "what if I wasn't hanging out with my boyfriend this weekend?" I give Micah what I hope is a flirtatious look. "Would you have something planned for us?" Maybe I should wink at him. Winking is flirtatious, right? It's what people do when they have a secret together. A secret that they don't want anyone else to know about.

"Then I would see if you wanted to hang out with me," Micah says. He pushes closer to me on the seat, and now he raises his eyebrows, like he's challenging me to say no or bring up my boyfriend again.

And then I get it. Micah doesn't like me. He just likes the idea that I might do something behind Brandon's back because of him. He likes the idea that he might win and get me to hang out with him. Wow. He's kind of a typical guy. Still, it's for the greater good.

"Well, maybe I could get out of hanging with my boyfriend," I say.

Or, you know, just make sure that Brandon doesn't want to hang out tomorrow night.

"Sounds good," Micah says. "So maybe tomorrow, after my mom's friend leaves, we could get together. We could go bowling or something. They have rock 'n' bowl at the lanes in town. You know, late night."

Yikes. Late night? That sounds serious. "Sure," I say, "I can do late night." As long as he's not talking about too late.

166

I mean, anything after ten and my dad is probably going to freak out.

"No!" Lyra says, sighing in exasperation. "You can't hang out with Micah late night! You need to get invited to the dinner so that you can see Rachel."

Oh. Right. I forgot about that part of it.

"Ah, maybe we could hang out earlier," I try. "My dad's not really a fan of me being out late."

"But I just told you that I have a dinner thing earlier," he says. He reaches back into his bag and pulls out another handful of popcorn. He stuffs it into his mouth.

"Well, maybe I could come," I say.

He tilts his head and thinks about it, but then he shakes his head ever so slightly. "I don't know," he says doubtfully. "It's not really going to be that fun."

I move a little closer to him on the seat, letting my arm brush against his on purpose. "Oh, I'm sure it will be fun, being with you," I say. "We can do both. I'll come over early for dinner, and then later we can go out, um, late night. That way we'll have plenty of time to get to know each other."

Oh my God. I am shamelessly flirting. Like, completely over the top, throwing myself at him. There's no way he's buying this, is there? I hardly know him. And besides, I have a boyfriend. How can Micah possibly think that a girl with a boyfriend who has only known him for, like, five minutes can be so excited at the prospect of spending a whole Friday night with him?

"Sounds good," he says. "I'll talk to my mom about it."

The bus pulls to a stop, and he stands up. "This is my stop," he says. He carefully folds up the now empty popcorn bag and hands it to me. "Throw this out for me, okay?"

And then he's gone.

Chapter

10

Friday passes by in a blur. I'm so nervous that I'm going to get caught talking to Micah that I totally ignore him at school.

Of course this somehow just makes him more interested. He keeps following me around, trying to talk to me. When I come out of gym, he's there. When I turn the corner by the library, he's there. He's always, you know, *lurking* around.

"Who are you looking for?" Ellie asks me as we're walking out of school at the end of the day.

"No one," I say, shrugging and trying to look innocent.

"Then why were you looking around?"

"No reason," I say.

"You better not be looking for that jerk Micah," Kyle says, coming up behind Ellie and putting his arm around her.

"I would never be looking for Micah," I say, aghast.

"Good," Kyle says. He puffs his chest out. "Because I wouldn't want to have to kick his butt."

Ellie giggles. I guess she thinks that Kyle getting into a fight is charming or something. Not that it would be much of a fight. I mean, Micah's an eighth grader. He's, like, twice the size of Kyle. It would be over in a second.

"You wouldn't fight him," Ellie says.

"Yes, I would," Kyle says. "I'd meet him at the flagpole and everything."

The flagpole is where everyone meets when they say they're going to fight. The sad thing is, it usually never happens. A big group of people will gather at the flagpole after school to watch whatever fight is rumored to be happening, and inevitably one of the participants ends up chickening out, and then everyone just stands there until a teacher comes and tells them all to move it along.

Ellie giggles again.

I'm not going to judge her for thinking it's hilarious that Kyle is getting all macho. I mean, I'm just glad I was able to explain to her about me being at the salon every day. I told her that I just felt really bad for Micah about losing his sister. That it reminded me of how my grandma died, only worse, since Lyra was our age.

But then I told her that it wasn't worth losing Brandon over, and that I wasn't going to do anything to jeopardize that relationship, so I knew I had to stop. She was skeptical at first, but by the end I started crying, and she totally bought it. I felt guilty, but only for a short while. All I have to do is get through this weekend, and then this whole thing will be over. I'll figure out what's up with Rachel and solve it. Lyra will be gone, and therefore Micah will be gone.

Well, not gone, exactly. But he'll be out of my life, at least.

"So what are you doing tonight?" Ellie asks me.

"Oh, I have to do my homework," I lie.

She frowns. "On a Friday night?"

"Yeah. I need to get it all done so that I have tomorrow free."

"Yeah," Brandon says as he joins our group. He takes my hand, and I feel a rush of warmth. "She needs to have the whole day free tomorrow. We have a date."

"Oooh," Ellie says. "How romantic. What are you guys doing?"

"It's a surprise," Brandon says, grinning. "I'm not telling her."

"How come you never plan a surprise date for me?" Ellie asks Kyle.

"I thought you said you didn't like surprises," Kyle says.

"Usually I don't," Ellie says. "But I'd like a surprise if it was from you."

"Yo, woman, I'll get you a surprise," Kyle says. "Whatever Kyle's woman wants, Kyle's woman gets."

Brandon and I look at each other doubtfully. Then he pulls me a few feet away so that we'll have some privacy.

"So my dad's going to pick you up tomorrow night at six," he says.

"Okay." I feel the butterflies start up in my stomach. Ever since Brandon told me he was planning a date for us, I've been looking forward to it. And now it's happening tomorrow. "Should I wear anything special?"

"You should dress up a little," he says. "But nothing too crazy."

"Like a dress?"

"Yeah, you could wear a dress. Nothing too fancy, though."

"Okay," I say, already planning to text Ellie as soon as I get on the bus and ask her to come over on Saturday and help me get ready.

"I should go," Brandon says, and then he leans down and kisses me. "But I'll text you later."

"Okay," I say. Hopefully, he doesn't text me while I'm over at Micah's house. That could be a little awkward. I mean, I'm going to be having dinner with Micah's family and everything. I doubt I'll be able to text. "If I don't text you back right away, it just means that I'm getting my homework done so that we can have our date tomorrow."

"Okay." Brandon squeezes my hand, and then he's gone.

I watch him make his way through the crowd of kids toward his bus. His navy blue backpack bounces behind him, and I get a little giddy watching him. How lucky am I that he's my boyfriend?

I turn around and start heading for my bus. As I do, I catch Madison Baker watching me from the other side of the parking lot.

Too bad for you, Madison, I think with a smile. *Everything's going great with me and Brandon, and you can't do anything about it.*

"You have to wear something cute," Lyra tells me later that night. We're in my room, and I'm getting ready to go over to her family's house.

"What's wrong with what I'm wearing?" I ask. I have on jeans and a light gray Henley shirt printed with purple butterflies. It's one of my favorite shirts. It's really pretty, and it has been washed so many times that it's super-soft.

"Nothing's *wrong* with it," she says. "But it's not exactly what you'd wear out on a date."

"It's not a date," I remind her.

"Not to you," she says. "But to Micah it is. And he's not going to want to keep you around if you don't at least make a little effort."

"Lyra," I say, rolling my eyes. "I am not going to get all

173

done up for your brother. If he doesn't like me the way I am, then that's too bad for him." Honestly, it doesn't matter what I look like. I mean, once I get there, he can't just kick me out of his house, can he? I can't imagine he'd take one look at me and then be like, *Um, you're not as cute as I wanted you to be, so you're not invited anymore.*

Although with boys you never know. They do crazy things all the time.

"Fine," Lyra grumbles. "But if you don't get the information that you need, then don't blame me."

"Whatever." It doesn't even matter what Micah thinks anyway, I tell myself as I pull my sparkly butterfly necklace out of my jewelry box and fasten it around my neck. What really matters is what Rachel thinks. Will she trust me enough to tell me why she's so upset about Lyra? That's going to be the big test. And she's going to be far more likely to talk to me if she thinks I look trustworthy and friendly and approachable.

I check the clock. Ten minutes to seven.

Micah and his mom should be here to pick me up any minute. Micah lives on the other side of the cemetery, and it would only take me about five minutes to walk there, but my dad doesn't like me walking through the cemetery after dark. Actually, he doesn't like me walking anywhere after dark.

So Micah's mom is coming to pick me up.

Of course, my dad doesn't know Micah's mom is coming to get me. He thinks *Ellie's* mom is coming to get me. And the reason he thinks that is because I told him I was going to Ellie's.

There's no way I could tell my dad I was going over to a boy's house, especially a boy who wasn't Brandon. First, he probably wouldn't let me go. Second, he would ask me all kinds of questions, like who the boy was and who else was going to be there, and could he meet the boy's parents, and what happened to Brandon, and blah, blah, blah.

So I just decided to tell him I was going to Ellie's house. Yes, it's a lie. And yes, I feel bad about it. But it's part of my job. Otherwise I'm going to be stuck with Lyra forever.

I grab my purse and throw my lip gloss into it.

"I thought you didn't care what you looked like," Lyra says as we head downstairs.

"I don't."

"Then why are you packing your lip gloss?"

"Just because I packed my lip gloss doesn't mean that I care about what I look like," I say. "I always wear lip gloss."

When I get downstairs, my dad and Cindy are watching a movie on the couch. And they're holding hands. Ew. I mean, I know I said I was okay with the whole my-dad-and-Cindy-being-together thing, but come on. Do they have to hold hands like that in front of me?

"Hi, Kendall," Cindy says, giving me a big smile. "Do you want to watch the movie with us?"

"Oh, no thanks," I say. "I have plans."

"Okay." She looks a little disappointed. Probably she wants to bond with me or something. The thought is kind of panic-inducing, if you want to know the truth. I don't really want to bond with Cindy. We really don't need to start hanging out and talking about boys and fashion, do we?

"I totally would," I say, to make her feel better, "if I didn't have plans." I squint at the screen, where two old people are holding hands and running on the beach. Wow. Looks like a real exciting movie. It's probably one of those ones about old people falling in love and then one of them dying. Why the heck would my dad and Cindy want to watch this?

"Well," she says, "maybe we could go to the mall or something this weekend."

My dad beams at her while I try to keep the horror I'm feeling inside from showing on my face. A day at the mall with Cindy? That sounds like a recipe for disaster. Although I guess now I'll probably have to do things like that with her from time to time. I should probably get used to it.

Hmm. I wonder if she'd be one of those nice step-mothers who would try to overcompensate for everything by buying me tons of presents. Not that I would ask for them. But there was a girl last year who got this really rich stepfather who would take her and her brother on all these great vacations and then bought her, like, four pairs of UGG boots and a Michael Kors watch.

I don't think Cindy is rich, though. At least, if she is, she doesn't show it.

"That could be fun," I say noncommittally.

I hear the sound of a car pulling into the driveway, and I glance out the window. Oh, thank God. It must be Micah and his mom.

"Okay!" I yell to my dad, hoping he's not going to get up and look out the window to see if it's really Ellie and her mom. "I'll see you a little later tonight. Enjoy the movie! No need to get up. You don't want to miss anything."

I cringe as the words come out of my mouth. I mean, could I be any more obvious? But my dad and Cindy don't seem to notice. They just wave and say good-bye, and then Cindy rests her head on my dad's shoulder.

Gross.

When I get to Micah's mom's car, she's unbuckling her seat belt.

"Hi," I say, sliding into the backseat.

"Hey, cutie," Micah says from right next to me. Yikes.

"Ugh, he's so obvious," Lyra says, appearing in the front seat.

I got into the backseat because I just assumed that Micah would be sitting in the front. Who sits in the backseat when there's an empty seat in the front? Unless he sat back here because he wanted to sit next to me. Or unless he just thought that *I* would sit in the front. Like he was saving the front seat for me to be nice.

But it's too late now. I'm already in the back. How ridiculous would it be if I got out and moved to the front? Plus Lyra's already up there. Ghost or not, it would be weird if I just sat on top of her.

"Doesn't your dad want to meet me?" Sharon asks.

"Oh, no," I say. "He's fine with me coming over."

"Are you sure? I don't mind popping in for just a second." She finishes unbuckling her seat belt and goes to open the car door.

"He's actually not home," I say, crossing my fingers that she buys it, even though half the lights in the house are on, his truck is in the driveway, and the stupid TV is on so loud that you can practically hear it all the way out here.

"Oh," Sharon says, shutting the door and buckling her seat belt back up. "Well, maybe he'll be here when I drive you back."

Or maybe not.

The whole ride to Micah's house, he's grinning at me and trying to hold my hand. At least, I think he's trying to hold my hand. When he got too close, I quickly slid my hand back into my lap.

I think he thinks I'm shy.

"Wow, this house is a disaster," Lyra says, shaking her head as we walk in.

She's kind of right. There are boxes all over the place, labeled with things like "Dishes" and "Books" and "Odds 'n' ends." Some of them are open, their contents peeking out of the top, like someone needed something inside but didn't want to take the time to actually unpack the box. But there are cozy-looking chairs in the living room, and the whole place smells like spiced apples.

"I like your house," I say honestly.

"This house needs to be organized!" Lyra yells. She starts peering into the half-open boxes. "I wonder what they did with my stuff," she mumbles. "They better not have donated it all to Goodwill. I had some really cute sweaters."

"Thank you," Sharon says. She looks around. "It's a bit of a mess right now, but hopefully, once we're all unpacked, it'll be nice."

"It's already nice," I say.

"I like her, Micah," Sharon says, grinning at us both. "You need to bring girls like her home more often."

Micah beams, like he's the one responsible for my politeness.

"Well," Sharon says. "I guess I should get back to the kitchen. I have sauce ready to heat on the stove, and I need to get started on the meatballs."

"Do you need any help?" I ask.

"No, no, I think I've got it all covered." She doesn't sound so sure, though. And now that we're inside in the light, I can see she has a big smear of tomato sauce on her cheek. Yikes.

"Well, okay," I say. "If you're sure."

"Of course I'm sure," she says. "You young people have fun and hang out." She shoos us over to the couch and then disappears into the kitchen.

Wow. I guess she doesn't really care about her son being left alone with a girl. It's, like, not even crossing her mind that maybe it's not the best idea. My dad would never leave me alone in a room with Brandon.

Maybe Sharon knows her son better than I think she does. Maybe Lyra has him all wrong. Maybe Micah isn't some kind of ladies' man, and Lyra just thinks that because he's her brother and people are always thinking bad things about their brothers. Maybe he's actually a really nice guy.

"Wanna watch a movie?" Micah asks.

"Sure," I say. "What do you have?"

"Eh, it doesn't matter," he says, then turns the TV on and starts flipping through the channels. He lands on one of those goofy movies that get their laughs from physical comedy, like the main character falling all over himself and pretending to trip and stuff. I hate movies like that.

"Maybe we should watch something else," I say. "Sometimes they play good movies on ABC Family on Friday nights."

But Micah either ignores me or doesn't hear me. Instead of responding or picking up the remote to turn the channel, he reaches over and dims the light.

And then he sits back down AND PUTS HIS ARM AROUND ME. Okay. Do not panic. Do. Not. Panic. Just because there is a boy who has his arm around me and I may or may not be cheating on my boyfriend right now doesn't mean that I should panic.

"Wow," Lyra says. "You're kind of cheating on Brandon right now."

"I am not cheating on Brandon," I mouth at her. It's true. I mean, just because I'm letting Micah put his arm around me does not mean that I'm cheating. It's all part of my job. In fact, I'm kind of like an actress who's playing a role, and in this scene a boy has to put his arm around me. It's like I'm in a school play or something. And if I were in a school play and this were happening, it definitely wouldn't be cheating.

"If you say so," Lyra says, shrugging. "Anyway, this is boring. I'm going to go check out the rest of the house. I'll be back when Rachel and her mom get here."

Great. Now I'm left alone with Micah. And yeah, even though Lyra's a ghost and no one can see her but me, it was still comforting to have her around.

"So, uh, have you seen this movie before?" I ask Micah. I shift away from him on the couch in an effort to make it too uncomfortable for him to keep his arm around me. But he just moves closer.

"I've seen it before, yeah," he says. Then he grins. "But I've never seen it with you."

"Oh," I say, dumbfounded. I'm trying to think of something witty and interesting that will make him stop looking at me like that, because honestly, I'm afraid he might try to kiss me. And let's face it, I can kind of bend the truth about him putting his arm around me, but if a kiss was to take place, that would definitely be cheating.

But before I know it, his lips are coming toward mine. I practically leap over to the other side of the couch.

"You like to play hard to get," he says, nodding.

Yikes. "Um, well, not really," I say. "I mean, I have a boyfriend."

"Well, he's not here right now, is he?" He grins at me again. I'm pretty sure he's just about to move in for another kiss when it happens.

The TV goes all weird.

Wavy white lines fill the screen, and the sound of static echoes through the room at a super-high volume.

"Whoa," Micah says. "What the heck happened?"

"Micah, turn that down," Sharon yells from the other room. "You're going to blow out the speakers."

Micah goes to turn it down, but it doesn't work. In fact, the volume just gets louder. And that's when I see her. Mrs. Dunham. She's on the TV. Like, her *face* is actually on the screen.

"Kendall," she says. "Stay away from my son. I'm serious this time. My patience is running out."

My blood runs cold and my heart starts pounding wildly in my chest.

I look over at Micah to see if he can see Mrs. Dunham too, but he's just frowning down at the remote, pushing buttons in an effort to get the volume to go down. "That's weird," he's saying. "It won't even shut off. This stupid thing is busted."

Mrs. Dunham starts talking again, repeating for me to stay away from Brandon, and her voice is getting louder and louder, until I'm at the point where I want to scream at her to shut up. You'd think she'd be happy to see me with Micah, but apparently she knows it's all a ruse. I put my hands over my ears to try to block out her voice, but it doesn't work.

The lights start to flicker on and off, and then sparks fly out of the back of the television. After a moment the lights come back on, but the TV screen goes completely black.

"What the heck was that?" Sharon asks, appearing in the doorway. The sauce is gone from her cheek, but now she has some smeared on her shirt. I hope she plans on changing before the company gets here. She looks at the black television screen. "Micah! I told you you were going to blow the speakers out."

"Mom, I didn't do anything," he says. He's still trying to turn the TV on, but it's not working. "We were just sitting here watching TV when all of a sudden the whole thing went crazy." He looks at me for confirmation.

"It's true," I say. "We were just watching a movie."

Sharon sighs and puts her hand to her forehead, like she can't deal with this right now. I mean, she's trying to cook dinner for a bunch of people. A broken television set is probably the last thing she wants to deal with.

"Okay," she says. "Well, I'll call someone about it tomorrow. I think it's still under warranty."

I breathe a little sigh of relief. If the TV is under warranty, then it won't be my fault that Sharon has to shell out a bunch of money to get it fixed. I doubt she has a bunch of money to shell out. Her nail salon obviously isn't doing that well.

But my moment of relief is short-lived. Mrs. Dunham was in their television set! I've never seen something like that before.

I shiver. She said her patience is running out. What does that mean? Is she planning to do something dangerous?

But before I can think about what Mrs. Dunham might have in store, the doorbell rings.

Rachel has arrived.

Chapter

11

Rachel looks nothing like I pictured her.

She's small and meek-looking, with shoulder-length brown hair. She's wearing a pair of jeans and a navy blue T-shirt, with no jewelry or makeup, and plain white sneakers. Her hair is parted in the middle, and she's holding a book in her hand. She's very pretty—she just doesn't look like the kind of girl Lyra would be friends with.

"What?" Lyra asks defensively. "I told you I wasn't always so glamorous."

"Nice to meet you," Rachel says to me. She shakes my hand, and I give her a big smile. She kind of dismisses me, though, once she realizes that I'm here with Micah. She's probably used to seeing all kinds of girls around Micah, and she probably thinks any girl who's with Micah isn't worth getting to know.

Well! Time to prove her wrong about that.

"So," I say, "I see you have a copy of *A Tree Grows in Brooklyn*."

"Yeah." She hugs it to her chest protectively, like I'm going to try to steal it or something.

"I love that book."

"Really?" She raises her eyebrows.

"Yeah," I say. "I think Francie's a really awesome character. I used to wish I could collect scrap metal and then take the money to the penny candy store and buy sweets like she does."

"Me too!" Rachel exclaims.

Lyra shakes her head. "See?" she says. "This is why we started growing apart."

"You guys started growing apart?" I ask. This is news to me. The kind of news that maybe Lyra should have mentioned.

"What?" Rachel asks.

"Nothing," I say. "Just, you know, talking to myself."

"She talks to herself a lot," Micah reports. He slings his arm over my shoulder. "Come on, babe," he says. "Let's go up to my room."

"Um, shouldn't we hang out with Rachel?" I ask. "We don't want to leave her on her own."

"It's okay," Rachel says, holding her book up. "I can read."

"No, no," I say. "That would be rude."

"This is boring!" Micah yells.

Wow. I had no idea he was so volatile.

"Maybe we can do something," I say. "You know, like, uh, play a game or something."

"The TV's broken," he says. "Remember? So we can't play a video game."

"We could play a board game," I say.

"I hate board games," Micah replies. He plops himself down on the couch and looks around, like he's trying to find something to amuse himself with. "Hey, maybe we could go somewhere!" he says finally.

"Like where?" I ask warily.

"Like the bowling alley. We were thinking of going later anyway, remember?"

"But isn't your mom cooking dinner?" Rachel asks.

He waves his hand like this fact is of no consequence. "That food isn't going to be done for hours. She's the slowest cook ever. Besides, she'll probably mess up whatever it is she's making and then have to start over. We'll be here all night."

"He's right," Lyra says, nodding.

"Well, okay," I say. "But who's going to take us to the bowling alley?"

Micah rolls his eyes. "We can walk," he says. "It's right on Main Street."

"Yeah, I know where it is," I say. "But it's dark out."

Micah grins. "Don't worry, babe," he says. "I'll protect you."

Great. I turn and look at Rachel, who's sitting on one of the chairs now, with her book open, reading. "Rachel, do you want to go to the bowling alley?" I ask.

"Nah, she wants to stay here and read," Micah says.

"I can answer for myself, Micah," she replies, glaring at him. She opens her mouth, and for a moment I'm almost positive that she's going to say she'll stay here. That's what I would do if I were her. No way I'd want to go out to the bowling alley with Micah and some girl he was with who I'd only just met.

But then she puts her book down. "Yes," she says, "I'd love to go."

"Great," I say. "It's all settled."

The walk to the bowling alley is kind of horrible. It's cold outside, and I didn't bring my jacket. You'd think that maybe Micah would offer me his, but nooo. He just pulls gloves out of his pocket and puts them on his own hands.

"What did I tell you?" he brags as we walk through the cemetery. "Did I tell you my mom would let us go?"

"You told us," I say grudgingly. Rachel rolls her eyes. It

was actually surprisingly easy to convince Sharon to let us all walk to the bowling alley. I thought she'd probably flip out when Micah asked her, but she didn't. She was sitting at the kitchen table with Rachel's mom, and they were flipping through some old photos or something and laughing while they drank wine.

She didn't even care that we were going to be out in the dark, walking on busy streets. Of course, I don't know why I'm surprised. Anyone who lets her son work at a nail salon when they're not even a certified nail technician is obviously pretty lenient.

"She always let him do whatever he wants," Lyra grumbles as we walk. "She always liked him more than me."

I resist the urge to roll my eyes. I'm sure she's exaggerating, and besides, I'm having a hard time mustering up any sympathy for her. She's the reason I'm even in this crazy situation to begin with. Not to mention that since she's a ghost, she doesn't even have to be cold or anything.

"This cemetery is kind of creepy," Rachel says.

"Oooh, you're afraid of ghosts," Micah scoffs. "What a baby."

"There's nothing to be afraid of," I say. "Ghosts don't usually hang out at the cemetery." She gives me a weird look. "Uh, at least from what I've heard."

I scan her, looking for any sign of a cell phone. The sooner I can get her phone, the sooner I can see what could possibly be in it that might be making her so upset, and the sooner I can solve this mystery and get the heck out of here. Maybe I can even be home in time to see if there are any good movies on ABC Family. Although all the good ones usually start at seven, and so I've probably missed them.

When we get to the bowling alley, Micah marches right up to the counter.

"There's three of us," he says. "Me, my date, and Rachel."

Wow. Talk about rude. And unnecessary. Like the bowling alley shoe clerk really needs to know who he's with. I hope she thinks I'm Rachel, and that Rachel is Micah's date. Ha-ha.

"What sizes?" the girl asks, bored by us.

We give her our sizes, and Micah pays for the three of us. Which I guess is nice of him.

"Thanks for paying for me," I say.

"Of course," he says. "This is a date, after all."

Rachel trails behind us, reading her book. This isn't going so well. I mean, I'm supposed to be bonding with her and finding out all her secret woes, not letting her read her book while Micah acts like some kind of Mr. Moneybags.

"Do you bowl a lot?" I ask her as we remove our shoes and start putting on the bowling shoes. I try not to think about how many people have worn these shoes and how many germs are probably lurking in them. I wonder if it would be lame to go and get the antibacterial spray I saw sitting on the counter and spritz my shoes.

"Not really," she says. "Me and Lyra used to go sometimes."

Now we're talking. "Oh, right," I say innocently. "That's Micah's sister, right?"

"Yes." She nods. "She died a few months ago."

"I know," I say. "That must have been really hard for you."

"It was very hard," she says quietly. She finishes tying her shoes and then picks up her book and starts reading. All righty, then. So I guess we're done talking about that.

I sigh and try not to get frustrated. I mean, I just met the girl. It's going to take longer than five minutes for her to open up to me. I just hope it doesn't take more than a night.

An hour later I'm starting to think maybe this is going to take longer than a night. Rachel has been buried in her book, and no matter how many questions I ask her, I'm not getting any closer to figuring out why she was crying and why Lyra can't move on.

"Just take her phone!" Lyra says. She peers at Rachel. "She's got to have it here somewhere."

It's probably in the small beaded bag she's carrying.

Not that I've seen the phone. Shouldn't she be checking her phone, like, every ten minutes, the way any normal person would?

I make a big show of pulling my own phone out of my bag and checking the screen. I have a couple of texts from Ellie from earlier, just asking me what I'm doing and how my paper is going. That's because I told Ellie that I was working on a paper for social studies and wanted to get it done tonight before my big date with Brandon tomorrow. It actually worked out well, because Ellie's having dinner with her grandmother tonight. So she couldn't hang out anyway.

"Wow," I say, real loud. "I just can't believe how attached I am to my phone. I, like, can't go five seconds without checking it."

"Maybe you should turn it off," Rachel offers helpfully. "Sometimes when I turn my phone off, it helps me unwind. It's like unplugging from technology."

"Yeah," I say. "Do you find that you're always checking your phone too? Or is it just me?"

She cocks her head, like she's taking the question very seriously. "I check it fairly often," she says. "But not that much. Not as much as I used to. When Lyra was alive, we were always texting."

"It's true," Lyra confirms. "We used to text, like, a hundred times a day. My mom would be totally shocked when she got the bill. She had to add unlimited texts to our plan and everything."

"Strike!" Micah yells as he throws his ball down the lane. For some reason he insisted on using a fourteen-pound ball, which is, like, the heaviest one you can get. He can barely lift it, and once he releases it, it ends up going careening down the lane toward the pins and then knocks a few of them over. Every time he throws the ball, he screams "STRIKE!" even though so far he hasn't gotten even one.

"Yeah, I love texting," I babble. "What kind of phone do you have?"

"The old Droid," she says.

"Do you like it?"

"Yeah."

"Can I see it?" I ask.

Rachel frowns. "Yeah, I guess." She reaches into her bag and pulls out her phone, then hands it over. I have it! The phone is in my hand! "Oh, cool," I say. I pretend I'm studying it, like maybe I'm interested in its features or something. But now what do I do? It's not like I can just start going through her phone and looking for evidence of something. "It's very, uh, lightweight."

"Rachel, it's your turn," Micah says sourly. He's mad that he didn't get a strike. "I'm going to order some fries," he says. "You want anything, babe?"

"Um, no thanks," I say. "You want anything, Rachel?"

"No, thanks." She stands up and gets ready to take her turn. She heads up to the alley and picks up her ball.

And then I realize I'm still holding her phone. I take a deep breath and push the button for her texts. Then I hold my breath and wait to see what I find.

Chapter

12

The first thing I notice is that there are tons and tons of texts from Lyra. I scroll through them. Wow. Talk about being loyal. Rachel must have saved all the texts Lyra sent to her when she was still alive. I wonder if I would save all of Ellie's texts if anything ever happened to her. Probably. I mean, it's a good way to remember your friend. But still. They're kind of clogging up her phone. Shouldn't she find a way to, like, print them out or something?

And then, while I'm holding the phone, it vibrates with a new text. I look down. Lyra looks over my shoulder.

It's a text from someone named Talia.

"Talia!" Lyra shouts. "Oh my God. I remember her! Talia's this super-annoying girl who I was friends with before I died." She frowns. "But what is she doing texting Rachel? Those two aren't friends."

I hover over the text, knowing it would be wrong to read it. But would it *really* be that wrong? I mean, it might have something to do with why Rachel's been crying at night, and why Lyra can't move on. I push the button to open it.

Hey, it's me again! Just wanted to let you know that Lyra only hung out with you because she felt sorry for you. Guess you'll have to pick out your own clothes now, loser! LOL.

Wow. Talk about harsh.

Lyra, who's still reading over my shoulder, immediately goes into a rage. "That's a lie!" she yells. "I never said anything about being friends with Rachel because I felt sorry for her. And so what if I helped her pick out her clothes once in a while? Everyone's friends help them put together outfits. It doesn't mean you're a loser."

It's totally true. Ellie and I always put together outfits and accessories.

Lyra tries to stamp her foot on the ground, but of course it doesn't make a sound.

Well, at least we know why Rachel was crying. Obviously this Talia person is sending her texts and harassing her. But why?

"What are you doing?" Rachel asks, coming back over to where I'm sitting. She snatches her phone out of my hand.

"Nothing," I say.

"Yes, you were. You were reading my texts!"

"No, I wasn't!"

"Yes, you were."

"No, I wasn't."

"Yes, you were." She crosses her arms over her chest. "And now you're lying about it."

I think about it and quickly assess the situation. This might be the only time I ever get to see Rachel, especially now. We haven't become fast friends the way I'd hoped, and we're definitely not going to after she found me snooping around in her phone. So I make a quick decision.

"Fine," I say. "I was snooping in your phone."

She shakes her head. "Pathetic." She sits back down and starts reading her book. Micah still isn't back from getting his french fries, and technically it's my turn to bowl, but instead I stay where I am.

"So can I ask you something about those texts?" I ask.

Rachel ignores me.

"Ask her why Talia's being a brat!" Lyra screeches. "Go on, ask her!"

"It's just that I noticed there were a lot of them coming from someone named Talia," I say.

Rachel stays silent.

"And, um, well, I couldn't help but read one, and it doesn't seem like she's a very nice person."

"It's none of your business," Rachel says. She turns the page of her book, but her fingers linger on the corner of the paper, playing with it nervously.

"Yeah, I understand." I think about how I can make this up to her, how I can possibly get her to talk to me after she caught me going through her phone. And then I have an idea. I reach into my own bag and pull out my own phone. "Here you go," I say, holding it out to her. "You can look at my texts if you want."

"Why would I want to do that?" she asks. But her eyes are off her book and on my cell.

"Because I did it to you." I shrug. "You know, an eye for an eye and all that. I mean, it's only fair."

"I wouldn't ever look in your phone," she says. "That would be a gross invasion of your privacy."

"Oh, come on," I say, waving the phone around in front of her in what I hope is a tempting way. "Don't you want to snoop?"

She slams her book shut. "Fine," she says. Then she takes my phone. "Who's Brandon?" she asks after a moment.

Oops.

"Um, my boyfriend."

"You have a boyfriend?" She has a disgusted look on her face, like she can't believe I'd be here with Micah when I have a boyfriend. You and me both, sister. I think about lying, but I already told her that Brandon was my boyfriend, and I don't want to lose her trust. Well, any more than I have already.

"Yeah," I say. "I have a boyfriend."

"Then why are you here with Micah?" She looks interested, but a second later she shakes her head and hands me back my phone. "Actually, never mind. It's none of my business."

"No, it's okay." I pause for a second and try to think of a good excuse as to why I would be here with Micah when Brandon's my boyfriend. Something that doesn't include "Because of Lyra's ghost." Finally I just settle for telling Rachel as much of the truth as I possibly can without seeming like a crazy person. "Well," I say. "When I met Micah at the salon, I thought he seemed nice. I knew that he'd just moved here and that his sister had just passed away. So I thought I would be his friend. It wasn't until later that I realized he wanted to be more than friends. Otherwise I never would have hung out with him."

She nods. "That makes sense. So does your boyfriend know you're here?"

I open my mouth, but luckily her phone vibrates again before I have the chance to answer. She looks down at the screen. She doesn't say anything, but her face starts to get scrunched up, and her jaw sets. And I'm not sure if I'm imagining it or not, but it looks like her eyes are welling up with tears.

"Was it Talia again?" I ask softly.

"Why is Talia saying mean things like that?" Lyra demands. "She is slandering and libeling my name! People go to jail for things like that."

I highly doubt that's true, but whatever. Let her get upset. I'd be upset too if someone was sending texts to my best friend, pretending I said mean things about her. And I'm actually alive.

Rachel slides her phone back into her purse.

"Why don't you just tell Talia to stop texting you?" I ask. "I'm pretty sure you can call the phone company and get a block on her number if you want." I know because one time my dad had to get a block on this guy who kept calling his phone, asking for Carl. It was a wrong number, obviously, but the guy wouldn't believe it. He thought my dad was Carl and was pretending not to be. I think Carl owed him money or something.

"You wouldn't understand," Rachel says. But she doesn't pick her book back up, and I have this feeling that she might be ready to talk about it.

"You know," I say, "sometimes it's easier to talk about things with someone you don't know. Because they can't judge you. And because you're probably never going to see them again."

"That's a horrible plan," Lyra says, disgusted. "I would never talk to someone I don't know."

But apparently Rachel doesn't agree with her. Because a second later she takes a deep breath and says, "It's complicated."

I nod. "Most things are."

"Those texts?" she says. "I . . . I kind of want them to keep coming."

"*What?*" Lyra asks. "Why? Ask her if she believes them! She better not believe them. And that Talia better stop. I'll go haunt her right now."

I almost laugh out loud at the thought of Lyra taking off to haunt some person and threatening them with a lawsuit when they can't even hear her.

"So what's the deal?" I ask.

Rachel sighs.

I just sit there, not saying anything, just waiting, giving Rachel the chance to tell the story in her own time, in her own way. And after a second she starts to talk again.

"So Talia, the girl who's sending those texts to me? She, um, she used to be friends with Lyra." But even as she's saying it, I can tell there's more to the story. I can tell because Rachel's voice gets really quiet, and she looks down at the floor of the bowling alley and starts blinking really fast, like she's trying to stop herself from crying.

And at the same time she's doing that, Lyra gasps. "Talia!" she says. "Oh my God, Talia!"

I guess she's remembering something. Figures that she

201

remembers it right when Rachel's about to tell me anyway.

"I ditched her," Lyra says quietly, staring at Rachel. "I ditched Rachel for Talia, because Talia was cool and popular."

"Talia's cool and popular," Rachel says, almost like she heard Lyra and is now echoing what she said. "And Lyra liked hanging out with her. At first they were just on the soccer team together. But then they started hanging out, and then they started hanging out more, and then Lyra started hanging out with Talia instead of hanging out with me."

God. That was really mean of Lyra. I raise my eyebrows at her, but she's not even looking at me. She's just staring at Rachel with a really sad look on her face.

"Okay," I say. "So why is this girl Talia texting you?"

Rachel shrugs. "Just to be mean. Talia was always jealous of me, which was crazy, since obviously Lyra was choosing her over me anyway."

"No, I wasn't." Lyra shakes her head. "I wasn't. I always thought I would have a ton of time to hang out with both of them, and then . . . well, I guess I ran out of time."

"So she's texting you just to be mean? I don't get it."

Rachel nods. "Yeah. I mean, I guess that's the reason."

But Lyra's shaking her head. "No," she says. "That's not the only reason. We had a fight. A day or so before I died. I remember now. I was yelling at Talia, telling her that I never should have ditched Rachel for her. That Rachel was a better friend than she ever was. Talia's probably still mad about it, and since I'm not there, she's taking it out on Rachel."

"Wow," I say, "that's a little cruel." And by "a little," I mean, you know, "a lot." I mean, who does that? "So why don't you tell someone? You could tell your mom, and I'm sure she'd help you do something about it."

"Yeah, I thought about doing that." Rachel gets really busy pulling at her hair.

"But?" I prompt.

"But . . . I told you, I kind of don't want them to stop." She looks at me, her voice shaking. Some of the color has gone out of her face.

"Why not?"

"Because I'm . . ." She trails off, and I get the feeling that whatever she's about to tell me is going to be really hard for her. She taps her foot on the floor nervously and twists her hands in her lap. "It's just . . . I feel like maybe Talia might be able to tell me what it was like being with Lyra for those last few days before she died. You know, like if Lyra was happy or not."

"Let me get this straight," I say, shaking my head. "You want crazy-mean Talia to keep texting you horrible things because you want to know what Lyra's last days were like?"

"Yeah." She swallows hard. "What?" she asks, jutting

her chin out. "You're the one who's on a date with someone other than her boyfriend."

"It's not a date," I say.

"Yeah," she says. "Tell that to Micah." She swings her feet under her chair and takes a deep breath. "Look, I know it's crazy," she says. "I just don't like thinking about how I wasn't with Lyra those last few days. She was with Talia, and I just . . . I wish she could have been with me."

"So you didn't talk to her in the days before she died?" I ask softly.

"No, not for a couple of days. I was away, visiting my aunt for the weekend, and when I got back . . . she was gone." Her eyes are really filled with tears now, and one slides down her cheek and drops off her chin. "And I read online that some of the heart stuff, like with the kind of disorder she had, can be caused by stress. And I knew that. But Talia didn't. And so I'm just wondering, if I'd fought harder for her, if I'd been the one hanging out with her that day . . ."

"If you could have stopped her from dying."

Rachel nods. She's full-out crying now, the tears streaming down her face. Even I'm getting a little choked up. I mean, let's face it—it's super-sad.

"No." Lyra shakes her head. "Go on, tell her she's wrong. Tell her it wouldn't have made a difference. Tell her Talia's a big jerk and I hate her."

"It wouldn't have made a difference," I say. "It wouldn't have stopped her from dying." I decide to leave out the part about Talia being a jerk, for now.

"How do you know?"

"Because," I say. "It wouldn't have."

"What are you two crying about?" Micah asks, walking back over to us. He's holding a cardboard container of french fries in his hand, and he picks one up, drags it through a pile of ketchup, and pops it into his mouth.

"I'm not crying," I say.

He looks at Rachel. "Well, why is she crying?"

"Can I tell him?" I ask.

She shrugs. I decide to take it as a yes.

"Because she thinks that if she'd been around your sister more before she died, she might have been able to save her life."

Micah shakes his head. "That's ridiculous. Lyra died because her heart condition was a lot more serious than anyone thought. No one could have stopped her from dying."

Rachel frowns. "But I read that her heart thing could be exacerbated by stress."

"Yeah," Micah says, "but like I said, what she had was a lot worse than the doctors initially thought when she was born. There was nothing anyone could have done for her."

"Are you sure?" Rachel asks.

"Yes, I'm sure. I'm her brother, for God's sake."

Rachel manages a small smile. And even though Micah is totally annoying, at that moment I want to hug him.

"You thought this whole time you had something to do with it?" he asks Rachel. "Because you didn't. It wasn't anyone's fault. Lyra would be really upset if she knew you were thinking that."

"She would?"

"Of course. She was always going on and on about how, no matter what, you would always be her best friend. She had a fight with that ridiculous Talia girl anyway. I'm pretty sure they were done being friends. And besides, Lyra always said, no matter what other friends the two of you guys had, you'd always be her *best* best friend." He thinks about it. "Which is a very girly thing to say, and I don't quite understand it, but whatever."

"Thanks, Micah," Rachel says, beaming.

"Feel better?" I ask her.

"I do."

"I have an idea," I say. I take my phone out of my bag. "What's Talia's number?"

"Oh, God," Micah says, rolling his eyes. "I only went on one date with her. You don't need to text her to find out about it. I'll tell you anything you want to know."

I look at him incredulously. Is this guy for real? Why would I care about his dumb date with Talia? I will be so glad when Lyra moves on and I can go back to my life. "This has nothing to do with you. Talia's been texting Rachel, being really mean and telling her all these bad things your sister was saying about her. Things that are obviously untrue."

"What?" Micah looks really mad. He sets his french fries down on the table that's in front of our alley and shakes his head. "My mom would freak out if she knew." He thinks about it and then nods. "Yeah, she should definitely call Talia's parents and tell her to cut it out."

"I don't want anyone's parents getting involved," Rachel says. She shakes her head and twists her hands in her lap. "Then Talia will just find another way to torment me, and probably even worse."

"You might not have to get her parents involved," I say. "What's Talia's number?"

Rachel hesitates, but then finally rattles it off. "Why?" she asks anxiously. "What are you going to do?"

"I'm going to take care of it," I say. I start to type a text into my phone. Lyra looks over my shoulder as I do it.

This is Lyra, I type. *I found out what you're doing to Rachel, and I am NOT HAPPY. Stop doing it or I will haunt you forever.*

The reply comes a second later, and it's just as I suspected. *Yeah, right. Get over yourself.*

I look at Lyra and raise my eyebrows. She knows exactly what I'm thinking.

"Tell her about how she kissed Simon Moncello at her party, and how I caught them and she made me promise not to tell anyone," Lyra says.

APOLOGIZE TO RACHEL, I type, *OR I WILL TELL EVERYONE HOW YOU KISSED SIMON MONCELLO AT YOUR PARTY.*

A second later Rachel's phone beeps. She reads the text and looks at me, her jaw dropping. "She said she's sorry," she says. "And that she won't do it again. How did you do that?"

"I told you to leave it to me," I say, smiling as I slip my phone back into my bag. Score one for me! And for Lyra.

I turn to give Lyra a high five. Or as much of one as you can give to a ghost. I don't even care that it's going to make me look totally crazy.

But when I turn around, Lyra's gone.

Now that Lyra has moved on, I'm actually able to relax. All I have to do is get through this night, and then there will be no more trips to the salon, no more lying to Brandon about why I'm there, no more lying to Ellie. And with everything settled, I'm actually able to start enjoying myself. Even Rachel starts to get into it.

We order some nachos and mozzarella sticks, and are just about to start on our second string of bowling when it happens.

I look up from high-fiving Rachel after I throw my first strike to see Brandon, Ellie, and Kyle walking into the bowling alley.

"Oh my God," I say, looking around wildly for somewhere to run.

But it's too late. I lock eyes with Ellie, and a second later Kyle turns to see what Ellie's looking at, and then *he* sees me, and then he elbows Brandon, and then the three of them are looking at me.

We all freeze, just staring at each other for what feels like forever but is probably only a few seconds.

Then Ellie glares at me and starts to come over. Kyle and Brandon follow her.

"Oh, hey, guys!" I say brightly. "What are you doing here?"

"What are *you* doing here?" Ellie asks. Wow. She looks really mad. Like, the maddest I've ever seen her, maybe.

"I thought you were doing homework tonight," Brandon says.

"I was," I say. "But, um, I decided to go bowling."

"You decided to go bowling after blowing off the texts I sent you?" Ellie asks. "The ones where I told you I was getting home from my grandma's house early and asking if you wanted to hang out?"

"Um," I say. "Well, it was the funniest thing. You see, I ran into Micah and—"

"Save it," Brandon says. "There's no way."

Ellie nods, then crosses her arms over her chest. Her eyes bore into me, and I'm so embarrassed that I have to look away. "Um," I say, "it's complicated."

Kyle shakes his head. "Not cool, Kendall," he says. "Not cool at all."

"Whatever," Ellie says. "If you want to lie to us, that's fine. But don't insult our intelligence by coming up with ridiculous excuses when you get caught."

And then, before I can stop them, they go walking to the other side of the bowling alley without looking back.

"Who was that?" Rachel asks.

"Just, um, some friends from school," I say, forcing a smile onto my face.

"That was her boyfriend," Micah says, slinging his arm around my shoulders. I duck out of his embrace and blink hard. The last thing I want is to start crying in front of everyone.

Micah shrugs and then walks back up to get his bowling ball. He tries to pull it off the little conveyer belt that returns the balls to you, but when he does, the belt reverses direction and his ball starts going backward down the track.

"Whoa, whoa, whoa," he says. He's trying to get his fingers out of the ball, but he can't. In fact, he's getting carried along with the ball, like the conveyer has a life of its own.

Finally he breaks free. "Jeez," he says. "Talk about being dangerous." He shakes his head. "We totally have to switch lanes."

And that's when I see her—Mrs. Dunham. She comes whooshing out of our alley from the back, where the pins are. Her energy must have started making the whole conveyer belt go wonky.

She starts jumping up and down on the lane faster and faster, twirling around happily in a circle before disappearing again. Obviously she's thrilled about what just went down between me and Brandon.

Suddenly I feel completely overwhelmed with how much of a big mess everything is. Ellie's mad at me. Brandon's mad at me. I might have lost my best friend and my boyfriend in the same night. And even if they weren't upset with me, it wouldn't matter. Mrs. Dunham is determined that Brandon and I shouldn't be together, so much so that she's willing to do anything to keep us apart. But why? Does it really have something to do with my mom? And if so, what?

I feel like the walls are caving in on me, like the whole room is spinning. I can't take it anymore.

"I think I'm going to go," I say to Rachel, gathering up my bag. "I, um, I'm not feeling good."

"You're not?" she asks. "What's wrong?"

"I think it's something I ate." I kick off my bowling shoes and slip my street shoes back onto my feet.

"Oh, no," she says. "Let's call my mom or Micah's mom to come and get us."

She goes to signal to Micah.

"No, that's okay," I say. "I can walk." And then, before she can say anything else, I'm running out of there.

When I get outside, the cool night air hits my face and instantly makes me feel better. But not too much. I start to head home, running as fast as I can. When I get inside, there's no sign of my dad or Cindy.

There's a note on the counter, letting me know that they couldn't find anything good on TV and decided to go out to a movie. For once I'm thankful they're on a date. That way I won't have to deal with them.

I head up to my room and change out of my clothes and into a tank top and a pair of pajama pants. I shut the light off and climb under the covers. It's dark and I'm in the house alone, but I'm not even afraid of Mrs. Dunham coming back. I'm too upset to feel anything else, even fear.

I start to cry then, and I cry so hard and for so long that my head feels heavy and I start to get a headache. I pull out my phone and text Ellie and Brandon both, telling them that I'm sorry and that I want to explain. But neither one of them texts me back.

I try to fall asleep, but I can't. I end up tossing and turning, kicking at my blankets. I hear my dad and Cindy come in at around eleven. They seem happy and chatty, and when my dad knocks on my door and peeks in to check on me, I pretend to be asleep.

At around two in the morning, when Cindy's long gone and my dad's in bed, and I'm still lying there staring at the ceiling and trying to fall asleep, I come to a decision.

I'm going to have to tell them. Brandon and Ellie.

I'm going to have to tell them everything.

I'm going to have to tell them about how I can see ghosts.

Chapter

13

I'm up and in the shower at eight the next morning. My dad's bedroom door is shut, and so I'm assuming he's still sleeping. That's good. I don't want him asking me questions about last night and what I did.

I dry my hair and then get dressed in jeans and a soft gray sweater. Then I sit on my bed and wait until the clock says nine o'clock. If Ellie isn't going to return my texts, then I'm going to have to go to her house and talk to her in person.

And even though I'm eager to get this over with, I think that showing up at someone's house before nine in the morning on a Saturday is probably pushing it. I want to show her that I care, but I don't want to come across as a stalker.

I write a quick note to my dad telling him I'm going to Ellie's for breakfast. Which isn't exactly a lie. I am going to Ellie's. Just not for breakfast. Although, maybe if we make up, she'll invite me in for a snack or something.

It's a little bit of a long walk to Ellie's house, and I'm anxious to get there as soon as I can, so I grab my bike out of the garage and start pedaling toward her house. It's cold out, and the wind nips at my face. Fall is in full effect, with no trace of summer left, a fact that's made all the more clear as my bike tires crush the leaves that are littering the sidewalk.

When I get to Ellie's house, I park my bike in her driveway, climb her brick steps, take a deep breath, and knock on the door. It's way too early for doorbells. I don't want to wake the whole house up.

"Kendall!" Ellie's mom says as she opens the door. "What are you doing here so early? Is everything okay?" She looks behind me, like she's half expecting me to be chased by kidnappers or something. She's not that far off— Mrs. Dunham is lurking in the bushes.

"Oh, everything's fine," I say. "I just wanted to see Ellie. Is she here?"

"No," Ellie's mom says. "I'm sorry, Kendall, but she went swimming at the Y with Brandon and Kyle."

"Oh, that's right." I snap my fingers, like I just forgot that's where she was, and not like the three of them obviously made some kind of plan without me. "I forgot that I was supposed to meet them there."

"Okay." She frowns, still looking a little confused and worried. "Would you like me to drive you?"

"No, that's okay," I say. "I have my bike." I scamper back down the steps before she can ask me anything else, especially, God forbid, if my dad knows where I am. Adults are always asking you if your parents know where you are. It's kind of annoying.

The Y is three miles away, and by the time I get there, the morning free swim is letting out. A bunch of kids are coming out the door, their hair still wet from the pool. I have no idea why Ellie, Brandon, and Kyle decided to go swimming this morning. They've never mentioned it to me before, so it must be something they just came up with last night. The thought of the three of them talking and making a plan, a plan that they were intentionally keeping me out of, makes my heart hurt.

I head into the Y. There's a big sign in the lobby that says FUND-RAISER FOR HAILEY THAYER TODAY. Hailey Thayer is a girl at the high school who had a kidney transplant last year. She's fine now, but she has a lot of medical bills that need to get paid.

I forgot that the Y was doing a fund-raiser for her. Kyle, Ellie, and Brandon must have decided to come at the last minute.

I peek into the pool area and see the three of them joking and laughing with a couple of other kids from our school. I take a deep breath and decide to wait out here. I don't think I should walk in there in front of everyone and ask Ellie if I can talk to her. But as soon as she comes out, I'll ask her if I can have a moment to talk to her alone.

I sit on a bench, swinging my legs under me, ignoring Mrs. Dunham, who's in the corner, glaring at me. I kind of want to glare back at her, because that's just the kind of mood I'm in, but I don't want to antagonize her. She'd probably start a tidal wave or something.

So instead I just sit there, inhaling the scent of chlorine that's wafting from the Y's Olympic-size pool, watching as people come out the locker room door and into the lobby in groups of twos, threes, and fours.

When Ellie, Brandon, and Kyle finally come out, they're talking and laughing. Ellie's hair is pulled back into a sleek ponytail, and her cheeks are rosy from exercise. Brandon's hair is still damp, and he's wearing a fleece pullover that makes him look so cute, my heart squeezes.

"Ellie," I say. I mean to call her name, but it comes out as almost a whisper. "Ellie," I try again.

She looks around, confused. But the smile on her face disappears when she sees that it's me. "Kendall," she says, walking over to me. "What are you doing here?"

"Your mom told me you were here," I say.

A look of guilt flashes across her face, and it gives me hope. If she's feeling guilty that she made a plan without me, then there might be a chance that we can be friends again. "We just decided to come last night," she says. "It was kind of a spur-of-the-moment thing."

I nod. I'm not going to give her crap for making a plan without me. I have no right to do that. And besides, that has nothing to do with why I'm here. "Hey, do you think we can talk for a second?" I ask.

"She doesn't want to talk to you," Kyle says, putting his arm around her. "You lied to her and made her sad."

I glance over at Brandon, who has moved a few steps away and is looking down at the ground.

I take a deep breath. "Ellie," I say. "Please? I have to tell you something really important."

She shakes her head. "I don't think so, Kendall," she says. "I'm really tired from swimming, and I kind of don't want to deal with this right now."

She turns around and starts to walk away, Kyle following behind her. I call her name, but she doesn't answer. My eyes fill with tears. So that's that. I really might have just lost my best friend. The thought of it burns deep in my soul.

I thought I was doing the right thing, but maybe I wasn't. Maybe I shouldn't have been helping Lyra move on to wherever it is she went. Or maybe I could have figured out a way to help her without lying to everyone who's important to me.

I would have dealt with Lyra haunting me forever if it meant that Ellie would still be my friend.

I turn away. I'm not going to follow them, because that would just be too humiliating. I'll wait until their ride shows up, and then I'll go outside and get my bike.

I sit back down on the bench and put my head in my hands, wondering how everything got to be such a big mess. Seriously, a month ago my life was—well, not perfect, but definitely not this much of a disaster. How did this happen? Maybe I need one of those life coaches. You know, the ones who help you navigate through your life when you're too messed up to do it on your own.

I'm just about to get up and check to see if the three of them have left yet when I feel someone sit down next to me.

I turn to look, my heart racing, hoping that it's Ellie, that she's come back to tell me that no matter what, we're always going to be friends, that she's mad now but of course she's going to listen to what I have to say.

But it's not Ellie.

It's Brandon.

My heart starts pounding even faster.

"Hi," he says softly.

"Hi."

He sets his bag down on the floor and then just sits there, not saying anything.

"Um, aren't you going to miss your ride?" I ask him.

He shakes his head. "Kyle's mom was picking us up. But I told them to go along without me, I'd walk."

"Oh." Brandon's house is way too far away to walk to. Especially when it's so cold out. Which means he must have really, really wanted to talk to me. Right? I don't want to let myself believe it, because if I do and it's not true, then I'm going to be crushed.

"Kendall," he says. "I think we really need to talk."

"Yes," I say, taking a deep breath. "We do."

He doesn't say anything.

I don't say anything.

"So, what's going on with us?" he says. "Do you still want to be my girlfriend?"

"Yes!" I say a little too loudly. "Yes, of course I want to be your girlfriend."

"So then why were you sneaking around last night with Micah?" he asks. He turns to look at me, and I can see the hurt in his eyes. I hate the fact that I hurt him.

"Brandon," I say. "There is nothing going on with me and Micah. I promise. In fact, I'm never going to talk to him again if you don't want me to."

He shakes his head. "I don't care if you're friends with him," he says. "But it doesn't seem like you guys are just friends. I mean, you keep lying to me about being with him."

"I know it looks bad," I say. I turn to him on the bench. A few more people come into the lobby, laughing and joking before heading out the front doors. I wait until they're gone before I talk again. "Do you want to go somewhere a little more private?" I ask.

"Like where?"

"We could go sit in the snack bar." I point through the double doors to the snack bar, where they're serving food and warm drinks.

He shrugs, and I decide to take it as a yes, so I get up and start walking inside.

Once we're at the snack bar, I order two hot ciders and bring them to a table in the back where Brandon is sitting and waiting.

"Thanks," he says, taking the drink from me.

"You're welcome." I take a sip of the hot cider, letting it slide down my throat and warm me. My hands are still cold from my bike ride, so I cup them around my drink. "So, listen," I say. "I'm going to tell you something now, and when I say it, you're not going to believe me."

Brandon frowns. "Why wouldn't I believe you?"

"Because it's going to sound crazy."

"Okay." He sets his cider down on the table, leans back in his chair, and waits.

"Um, so do you want to hear it?"

"I'm waiting, aren't I?"

"Okay." I wipe my palms on my jeans nervously. Wow. I thought there'd be more back-and-forth, like maybe I'd have to convince him to actually listen to me. Now that he's just going to let me talk, I'm a little nervous. I haven't prepared what I'm going to say or anything. I haven't thought about how to frame it. Should I just blurt it out?

"So this is going to sound crazy," I start.

"Yeah," Brandon says. "You already said that."

I have to stop stalling and tell him the truth.

"So, the reason I was hanging out with Micah," I say, "is because I was helping his sister."

Brandon's forehead crinkles in confusion. "His sister?"

"Yes. Her name's Lyra. She's the same age as us, and she was having problems with one of her friends."

"Was his sister that girl you were with at the bowling alley?" he asks.

"No," I say. "That was Rachel. She's Lyra's friend."

Brandon shakes his head. "I'm confused."

"I was at the salon," I say, "and that's where I met Lyra. She told me that she needed me to help her work out this problem she had with her friend."

"Why did she need you to help her?" he asks. "And why didn't you just tell me that?"

"Well," I say slowly. "That's the unbelievable part." I take a deep breath. "Brandon, Lyra's dead." The statement hangs in the air between us, the last word echoing through the almost empty snack bar.

"What do you mean, she's dead?"

"I mean she's a ghost." I swallow. "I can see ghosts."

He just stares at me. He's not saying anything. I study his face for clues about what he's thinking, but there's nothing. Just complete and total blankness. I take this as a good sign (at least he's not freaking out, right?) and so I push on.

"I've been able to see them since I was a little kid," I say, "and I help them to move on. So that's why I had to hang out with Micah. I needed to get closer to him so I could get closer to his sister."

He's still not saying anything, except now he looks stunned.

"Brandon," I say, "say something."

He shakes his head. "I don't . . . I mean, I'm not sure exactly what to say."

"Do you believe me?"

"I'm not . . . I mean, I don't . . ." He sighs. "You realize how ridiculous this sounds, right?"

I nod. We sit there for a few more minutes, neither one of us saying anything.

"Brandon?" I finally say in a small voice.

"Yes?"

"There's one more thing."

"What?" He sounds wary.

"I've also . . . um, I've also been seeing your mom."

He frowns. "My mom?"

"Yeah. She keeps showing up, telling me to stay away from you."

His face loses some of its color, and he holds on to the side of the table, like he can't believe what he's hearing.

"You can see my mom?" he asks in a small voice.

I nod. "Yes," I say. "She's always asking me to stay away from you. I don't know why."

He shakes his head, and his grip on the table gets tighter. I can see his knuckles turning white from the strain.

"Do you have any idea why she'd want to keep us apart?" I ask.

He nods. "Maybe it's because of what you're doing right now," he says.

"What?" His words feel like a slap.

He stands up and grabs his gloves off the table, and shoves his fingers into them angrily. "I knew something was going on with you and Micah," he says. "But I never thought you'd make up something like . . . to *lie* about being able to see my mom . . ."

"I'm not making it up!" I say. "Brandon, I would never—"

"Save it," he says.

And then he walks out on me.

· · ·

I sit there for twenty minutes or so, drinking my apple cider and trying to stop my hands from shaking. I told Brandon my secret. And he thinks I'm a freak. If I was worried about him never talking to me again before, he's definitely never going to talk to me again now.

I wonder if he'll tell Ellie. I wonder if she'll think I'm a horrible person too, for making up such a terrible lie involving someone's dead mother.

After a little while I'm done with my cider, and the girl working the counter is starting to give me dirty looks. I think they're closing or something.

So I get up and toss out my empty paper cup, then throw away Brandon's full one.

I get outside and hop onto my bike. Tears are dripping down my face, and even though it's cold outside, my whole body feels warm and heavy. I don't think I have the energy to even ride my bike home. But what choice do I have?

I can't call my dad and ask him to come and get me. He'll know that I lied to him.

I push off down the road. My feet feel like lead. I put my bike into the highest gear, but it doesn't really help that much. The adrenaline and hope that kept me going on the ride here are gone, and now all I feel is sad and tired.

But as I keep going, something starts to happen to me.

My sadness and fear start to turn into anger. Why am

I the one who has to devote her life to helping all these ghosts? Why should I not be allowed to have a normal life?

It's not fair!

I'm so angry that by the time I get to the cemetery, the pedals of my bike are flying. In fact, I'm so worked up that I keep going and going, past my house and all the way down Main Street. It's like I'm a woman possessed.

I don't realize exactly where it is that I'm going until I pull up in front of the bus station. I'm a little surprised that I'm here, but not really. I suppose that on some level, somewhere in the back of my mind, I knew it was going to come to this.

I'm going to have to get answers.

And there's only one person who might have those answers.

About Mrs. Dunham, and about everything else.

My mom.

Chapter

14

When I get to the ticket counter, I act like I know exactly where I'm going and pretend that I'm super-impatient to get there, just in case anyone gets suspicious that I'm traveling by myself. But to my surprise, the clerk doesn't care.

He sells me a ticket to Camden. The bus leaves in forty-five minutes.

I hold my breath as he swipes the emergency credit card my dad gave me (if this isn't an emergency, then what is?), but it goes through with no problem.

While I wait for the bus, I buy a Snickers bar and an orange juice. I drink the orange juice but only manage to eat about half the candy bar. Which is good. I'm hopped up enough already.

By the time I climb into the bus, I'm feeling surprisingly calm.

I even make conversation with the girl sitting next to me, a college student who's on her way home for a visit.

I expect the ride to feel like it takes forever, but it's actually the opposite. When the bus pulls into the Camden station, it seems like it's too soon.

There's a line of cabs waiting outside, and I climb into one of them.

I recite my mom's address, the address I pretend to care nothing about but memorized as soon as I saw it.

A few minutes later the cab pulls up in front of a suburban house with white shutters. It's a colonial, and there's a red Toyota parked in the driveway.

I peer out the window.

"Can you wait here?" I ask the cabbie. "Um, just for a minute? I might need you to take me somewhere else."

Now that I'm here, I'm starting to realize what a horrible plan this is. One, I don't even know if my mom still lives here. Two, I don't know anything about her life. Is she remarried? Does she have other kids? Is she going to slam the door in my face?

I pay the cabbie for what I already owe, swiping my emergency credit card through the machine and adding an extra-big tip, since he's willing to wait for me.

Then I make my way up the driveway. My anger is

gone, and now I'm just going on straight adrenaline.

I ring the doorbell, moving back and forth, shifting my weight from foot to foot. I have so much nervous energy, I think I'm going to explode.

After a moment the door opens.

And there she is.

My mom.

She looks exactly like I remember. Or at least I think she does. I'm not sure if I really remember her or if I just remember her from pictures. There are little wrinkles around her eyes now, and her hair is lighter. But she looks pretty. She's wearing a soft-pink sweater and a pair of white jeans.

She looks like me.

Her eyes brighten as soon as she sees me, her features arranging themselves into a shocked expression.

"Kendall," she says.

If I was worried about her not recognizing me, I guess I didn't have to be.

I nod, not knowing what to say.

"Do you want to come in?" she asks.

I stand there for a second, unsure.

She hesitates, then says, "I know why you're here." She takes a deep breath. "You're here because of Brandon."

And that's what settles it.

I move through the open door and into the front hallway. . . .

Check out Kendall's next adventure!

GHOST OF A CHANCE
By Lauren Barnholdt

This definitely might be the most horrible idea I've ever had. Like, *ever*. And let's face it, I've had some pretty horrible ideas. I mean, my life is kind of a mess right now.

Case in point:

1. I've told the maybe love of my life, Brandon Dunham, that I can see ghosts. Yes, it's true that I can see ghosts, but why, why, why would I tell him that? Am I crazy? What *good* did I think could possibly come of it? Especially since one of the ghosts I can see is his mom.

2. After I told Brandon about the whole seeing-ghosts thing, he accused me of lying, and then he left me sitting in the snack bar of the YMCA. Which I'm pretty sure means we've broken up.

3. After he left, I decided I should go see my mom. Now, I know what you're thinking—why is going to see your mom on a list of things that have turned your life into a big horrible disaster, Kendall? If I were a normal girl with a normal relationship with my mom, going to see her wouldn't be on this list. But I'm not a normal girl. And I don't have a normal relationship with my mother. I see ghosts. And I haven't seen my mom since I was a baby.

Anyway, the reason I had no choice but to go see my mom is because the ghost of Brandon Dunham's mom keeps showing up and threatening me, and then I found out that *my* mom and Mrs. Dunham were best friends when they were younger. So I had to come see my mom so I could ask her if she has any idea why the heck Mrs. Dunham won't leave me alone.

And now here I am, following my mom down the front hallway of her house. A house I've never been to. A house I've never even *seen*. So. Weird.

"Do you want some tea or something?" she asks as we walk into the kitchen. She opens the fridge and looks inside. "I didn't know you were coming. Otherwise I would have picked up some food. . . ."

"Tea would be great," I say. I don't really like tea, but whatever. I mean, we need to have something to do, don't we? We can't just be sitting here, having what is sure to be an awkward conversation, without something to eat or drink.

"Go ahead, have a seat," my mom says.

I slide my arms out of my coat and drape it across the back of a kitchen chair. It's a nice house, I decide. It looks big from the outside, but inside it feels cozy and warm. There are green-and-white-striped place mats on the table, and the chairs are the kind with cushions on them.

The chairs in my kitchen at home don't have cushions. In fact, now that I think about it, the chairs at my house are extremely uncomfortable. They force you to sit ramrod straight. I've never really thought about it before, but now I wonder, if my mom had been living with us this whole time, would she have made sure we always had comfy chairs?

"Here you go," she says, putting a mug of tea down in front of me.

"Thanks." I take a sip. It's so hot that it burns my tongue.

There's an awkward pause, and I really can't even look at her, because it's way too weird. I mean, what am I supposed to say? What am I supposed to do? The silence stretches on for another moment.

"I like your house," I say.

"Thank you."

"You're welcome." I swallow and feel emotions swirling through me. I want to ask her the question I've always wondered, the only thing I really want to know about her life. "Do you . . . Are you . . . I mean, do you live here alone?"

She nods.

"You're not married?"

She shakes her head.

"And you don't have any kids? I mean, uh, besides me."

"No." She's looking right at me as she says it. I let go of the breath I've been holding and feel the tightness in my chest loosen just a little. I don't want to know anything else about my mom, about her life, about what she does for a living or whether or not she's happy. She doesn't deserve my curiosity.

But I had to know if she had a new family. If she did, I don't think I'd ever be able to forgive her. For her to have left me is bad enough—but for her to have left me and then started another family would be much worse.

There's another short silence, like maybe she's waiting for me to ask her more questions about her life. But there's no way I'm going to do that. I didn't come here to find out about her. I came here for answers.

"Kendall," she says finally, wrapping her hands around the mug in front of her. "I know why you're here."

"You do?"

She nods and then sighs. "I'm sure you have a lot of questions. But you need to know that I may not be able to answer all of them."

"What do you mean?" I pick up my cup of tea, blow on it, and take another sip.

"What I mean is that there might be some things that you have to figure out on your own."

I bite back a laugh. It's kind of hilarious that she's saying that, since I've had to figure out things on my own for pretty much my whole life. Like how to talk to boys, how to put on makeup, how to dress, how to pretty much do everything girls need to know that their dads can't teach them.

"Yeah, well, wouldn't be the first time," I mutter under my breath. It's completely petty and immature to mutter under your breath, but I'm in a petty and immature kind of mood.

She opens her mouth to say something, but then thinks better of it. "That's fair."

Which just makes it worse, because at least if she was making excuses and trying to justify the fact that she left when I was little, I could blame her and yell at her. But her saying it's fair takes the wind out of my sails.

Okay, Kendall, I tell myself. *You need to take control of this situation.* This isn't one of those sappy reality TV shows where someone is looking for their long-lost relative, and then, once they find them, they start working on repairing their relationship. (Even though I totally love those shows. Honestly, who doesn't? They always have happy endings, which is completely the opposite of real life. Even though they call them reality TV shows, which is kind of ridiculous.)

"Look," I say, sitting up straight in my chair and looking my mom right in the eye. "I didn't come here for some kind of big reunion scene. I came here because I need to know about you and Julie Dunham."

She nods, like she expected this. Which makes no sense. How can she know I would show up wanting to know about Brandon's mom? Unless my dad called her and told her I was asking him questions about Julie Dunham.

Ohmigod. That must be it! My dad and my mom have been talking behind my back! It makes sense. Think about it. My dad had a girlfriend he never told me about, so who knows what kind of other scandalous things he's been hiding from me. Maybe my parents even met for coffee, and now they're going to end up—

"Julie Dunham and I were friends," my mom says. "Best friends, really. We were like sisters. We did everything together, and then we—"

"Wait a minute." I hold up my hand to stop her. "How'd you know I was going to come here and ask you about Julie Dunham?" I slip my other hand into my bag and get ready to pull out my cell phone. If my dad thinks he can just call my mom behind my back and I'm going to be cool about it the way I was about his secret girlfriend, well, then he's got another thing coming. I'll call him right here, and the three of us will get this whole thing out on the table.

"Because," my mom says, looking surprised, "I can see ghosts too."

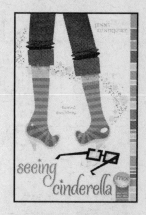

DOUBLE TROUBLE
JUST TOOK ON a WHOLE
new meaning....

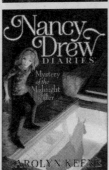

Enjoy these sweet treats from Aladdin.

FROM ALADDIN